The Vengeful Deputy

The town of Lone Ridge was a lawless hell-hole until the ruthless Nyle King eliminated all the gunslingers. Now Nyle controls the town and everyone who opposes him ends up dead, so US Marshal Caine tasks his deputy Gabriel Flynn with bringing Nyle to justice.

Gabriel goes to Lone Ridge, but only because he's searching for the outlaw who killed his brother, and believes Nyle may be the key to finding him. But Nyle claims that the recent deaths in town aren't his work and that someone is trying to frame him.

No longer knowing who to trust, the only thing Gabriel can be sure of is that hard lead alone will unmask the guilty and let him finally have his vengeance.

The Vengeful Deputy

I.J. Parnham

A Black Horse Western

ROBERT HALE

© I.J. Parnham 2018
First published in Great Britain 2018

ISBN 978-0-7198-2786-0

The Crowood Press
The Stable Block
Crowood Lane
Ramsbury
Marlborough
Wiltshire SN8 2HR

www.bhwesterns.com

Robert Hale is an imprint
of The Crowood Press

The right of I.J. Parnham to be identified as
author of this work has been asserted by him
in accordance with the Copyright, Designs and
Patents Act 1988

Typeset by
Derek Doyle & Associates, Shaw Heath
Printed and bound in Great Britain by
4Bind Ltd, Stevenage, SG1 2XT

CHAPTER 1

'We're obliged for your hospitality,' Gabriel Flynn said. He laughed and shook the bulging bag of stolen money. 'Now don't make the mistake of coming after us.'

'I won't need to,' the post-owner, Wilson Faulk, snarled with defiance in his eyes. 'After raiding my trading post you'll have got yourself a whole heap of enemies.'

'Who?'

Wilson bit his bottom lip, suggesting he now regretted making his taunt.

'For a start there's US Marshal Caine.'

Gabriel winced and he was about to ask for more details, but Lorenzo Moretti called out from the door.

'Stop wasting time back there,' he said. 'We need to ride.'

'I know, but Marshal Caine is around,' Gabriel said.

Lorenzo stormed across the trading post to face Wilson over the counter.

'Where is this marshal?' he demanded.

'I don't know, but he passed through on his way to Lone Ridge yesterday,' Wilson said. He lowered a hand to point at Lorenzo. 'So the moment he hears about what you did here he'll come for you. You varmints won't stand a chance.'

'I reckon we'll survive for longer than you will.'

Lorenzo licked his lips as he let his threat register. When Wilson gulped, he snapped up his gun arm and blasted a shot into Wilson's chest that made him stumble forward and double over to lie sprawled over the counter.

Gabriel watched in horror as Wilson twitched and then became still.

'You didn't need to do that,' he said.

'That's what happens to people who annoy me.'

Lorenzo directed a long glare at Gabriel, who nodded and hurried to the door. Outside, the third member of the gang, Emmett Barclay, was already mounted up.

'What happened in there?' Emmett said as Gabriel

and Lorenzo reached their horses.

'The post-owner annoyed Lorenzo,' Gabriel said. 'He told us that Marshal Caine will be coming for us.'

Gabriel mounted his horse and looked around, as if he feared that the lawman could appear at any moment.

His action made Lorenzo and Emmett consider both directions along the base of Jackson's Pass that led to the Hanging Rock trading post and then the high points to either side, including the huge boulder that stood halfway up the side of the pass.

Emmett shrugged. 'I've never heard of him, but if he takes us on, it'll be the last thing he does.'

'Don't be so confident. The marshal is a formidable lawman. We need to be careful.'

Emmett nodded, but Lorenzo narrowed his eyes.

'How do you know about this lawman?' he said.

'I've come across him before,' Gabriel said.

'And yet you've never mentioned him.'

'I didn't say anything because until a few moments ago I didn't know he was in the area.' Gabriel gestured ahead. 'Now are we going to stand here until he finds us or are we going to Cartwright's Gulch?'

Gabriel's impudence made Lorenzo sneer, but he couldn't argue with his suggestion, so he shook the reins and galloped away from the trading post. Emmett filed in behind him while Gabriel brought up the rear.

They had agreed on their escape route beforehand and Gabriel expected that Wilson's revelation would make Lorenzo change his plans, but when they emerged from Jackson's Pass he still headed for Cartwright's Gulch.

It took them thirty minutes to reach the entrance to the gulch where Lorenzo called a halt. They all turned to look back towards the pass.

The plains were devoid of movement, but then again it was unlikely that anyone would be following them so soon after the raid. The trading post was twenty miles out of Lone Ridge and before they'd robbed him, Wilson had reported that they were the first customers to visit him that day.

With that in mind, Gabriel didn't expect that they would have got away with much money, but when they grouped up to take a longer look at what they had collected, they all whistled with surprise. Gabriel had a bag filled with bills while Emmett had a small box that was brimming with silver coins.

Most surprising of all was Lorenzo's haul of gold and silver trinkets.

'That sure is a lot from such a run-down place,' Emmett said, speaking for them all.

'That's why I said we should raid the Hanging Rock trading post,' Lorenzo said with his chin raised, although his sideways glance at Gabriel confirmed that the result had surprised him as much as it had surprised Emmett and Gabriel.

Gabriel passed up the opportunity to mention that one of Lorenzo's contacts had suggested that they target Wilson and instead he turned back to face the gulch.

'So, are we still heading through there?' he said.

'Marshal Caine will be behind us, not ahead, so I see no reason to change our plans, but we'll keep an eye out for trouble.'

With that, Lorenzo turned his horse and trotted into the gulch. Gabriel again slipped in at the back and even with the group now riding at a more cautious pace, he let Lorenzo and Emmett draw ahead.

They wended their way along the winding pass. As Lorenzo and Emmett were looking to either side for trouble, nobody looked back at him.

They had covered three miles and had reached a point where the gulch was straight for a long stretch when Emmett grunted a warning and drew his horse to a halt. A moment later a strident voice echoed across the gulch.

'This is Marshal Caine,' the voice intoned. 'Raise those hands, get down off your horses, and surrender.'

Emmett must have spotted where Caine had holed

9

up as he drew his gun and raised it to aim at a spot high up on the side of the gulch, but before he could fire a gunshot blasted out. Emmett flinched back, a hand rising to clutch his bloodied chest before he toppled over backwards from his horse.

'Ambush!' Lorenzo shouted while turning his horse to head back towards Gabriel.

Lorenzo took in the sight of Gabriel, who was now over a hundred yards away. He still gestured at him to join him in fleeing, but Gabriel stopped and turned to face the area where Caine was hiding.

Gabriel drew his gun and fired two quick shots into the rocks above Caine's position. Then he beckoned for Lorenzo to hurry as gunfire peppered down at the bandit leader from the other side of the gulch.

Two men had fired at him, and Lorenzo swung round in the saddle to return fire. He loosed off a shot while Gabriel again fired high towards Caine's side of the gulch.

While he appeared to mount a defence, Lorenzo stopped and faced in the opposite direction. He managed to blast off another shot but as he was not moving, one of his opponents got him in his sights and a gunshot to the chest made him slump forward. Then a shot in the back made him slip from his mount and fall to the ground.

Gabriel sighed and holstered his gun. With slow

movements he got down off his horse and walked ahead for a few paces.

He watched the other two men. They were both still and so Marshal Caine stood up and gestured, ordering two deputies to stand up on the other side of the gulch.

All three men moved down to the base and while the deputies checked on the bodies, Caine headed towards Gabriel. He stopped before him and looked him over.

'Howdy, Deputy Flynn,' he said with a smile. 'You did well.'

'Again,' Gabriel said, returning the smile.

Deputy Edgar Newhall bustled into the law office to find that Sheriff Morrison was leaning back in his chair with his feet on his desk as he enjoyed a siesta. The sound of him hurrying in made Morrison stretch and raise his hat.

'You look concerned,' Morrison said.

Edgar nodded and pointed outside. 'I've just found a body behind the Silver Palace saloon.'

Morrison winced as he slipped his feet off the desk.

'Then I guess we should check out this body.'

He directed Edgar to lead the way and so they headed outside. It was late afternoon in Lone Ridge and even though few people were outside, the two lawmen walked in a casual manner so as not to imply that anything was amiss.

When they reached the back of the saloon nobody other than the body was in sight. The two men took in the scene before Edgar explained the situation.

'Bart White heard an argument going on behind his mercantile. Then later he heard a gunshot. I checked it out, but nobody was around and so I scouted around until I came across this.'

Morrison moved to stand over the body, his stern gaze noting that the man had been shot in the face, the angle of the bullet creating a wound that was so disfiguring Edgar had been unable to make out his features. He knelt beside the twin furrows trailing away from his feet.

'These marks and the lack of blood on the ground suggest that he was killed elsewhere and then dragged here.' Morrison shrugged. 'So I reckon this incident didn't have nothing to do with Nyle King or his saloon.'

'We can't assume that,' Edgar said. 'Bart reported that when he heard the argument the men were coming from this direction. Worse, the victim's been shot in the face and he's the second man to die like that and been left behind the saloon this month.'

Morrison tipped back his hat as he thought this

12

through and then nodded. 'Go and fetch the under-taker. Then question Bart again and see if he can remember anything more.'

'Sure, and you'll question Nyle?'

Morrison grunted in a distracted way and then stood up to walk around the body. Edgar stayed for a few moments, but when it became clear that Morrison no longer needed his help he moved on.

He headed back to the main drag and then along the boardwalk to Samuel Buckhorn's workshop. When he looked through the window of the under-taker's, he saw that Samuel was talking with someone so he dallied outside the doorway.

While he waited, Morrison came around the other side of the saloon and walked towards the door where he stopped. Edgar could understand his reluc-tance in again having to see Nyle to discuss another body that looked as if it might be connected to his saloon, but which Nyle would probably dismiss as having nothing to do with him.

Morrison glanced around. Then, with a roll of the shoulders, he turned on his heels and walked away from the saloon.

Edgar watched Morrison until he was sure that he was in fact returning to the law office and then headed into the workshop.

CHAPTER 2

'Emmett Barclay was just as much trouble as Lorenzo Moretti was,' Marshal Caine said when he'd confirmed with his deputies, Thorpe and Raul, that the two outlaws were dead. 'So I won't blame you because we couldn't take them alive.'

'Of course you shouldn't,' Gabriel Flynn said. 'I did everything you asked of me. I got close to Lorenzo, earned his trust, and gave you the details of his raid. It was you who made a mistake when you visited the post yesterday. Wilson told Lorenzo about you. Without that warning he might not have been edgy and you'd have been able to arrest him.'

Caine shook his head. 'I had to check out the area beforehand and I don't reckon that did any harm.'

'Tell that to Wilson,' Gabriel snapped, advancing

on Caine. 'Lorenzo killed him when he mentioned you.'

Caine shrugged and raised an eyebrow, seemingly surprised by Gabriel's reaction.

'Then that saves me the trouble of having to arrest Wilson.' Caine waited until Gabriel furrowed his brow and then smiled. 'Didn't you wonder why you gathered such a large haul from a place that barely had any customers?'

Gabriel sighed and lowered his head for a moment.

'I guess that was strange. Even Lorenzo was surprised, except clearly you aren't.'

'I'm not. Most things that got stolen in Lone Ridge ended up at the Hanging Rock trading post before they were sold on. So our mission dealt with two problems.'

Gabriel narrowed his eyes. 'I didn't know that. You only told me about Lorenzo and that omission could have ruined the mission.'

Caine considered Gabriel and then spread his hands.

'You're right. I should have told you the full story. I'll make sure I do that the next time.'

Gabriel shook his head. 'There won't be no next time. We had an agreement and that was my last mission for you. Now give me the name of the man who shot my brother and we can part company on good terms.'

'This *is* our final mission together, but it's not over yet. Lorenzo and Wilson weren't the men we were after. They're just small men who'll lead us to the big prize, Nyle King.'

Gabriel rubbed his jaw. 'Nyle runs the Silver Palace saloon in Lone Ridge?'

'He does, along with just about everything else in town, and he's behind most of the local trouble, except he's careful and nobody can ever prove nothing. Sheriff Morrison claims he'll bring him to justice, but I reckon he has neither the guts nor the inclination to do it. I have both, and you're going to help me.'

Gabriel frowned. 'Maybe if you'd told me that at the start I'd have accepted it, but you've strung me along for too long. We part company now.'

Caine licked his lips, seemingly enjoying their discussion despite Gabriel's ultimatum.

'That's not your decision to make. I appointed you as my special deputy and that duty ends only when I say so.'

Caine turned away and moved to join Thorpe and Raul, so Gabriel hurried forward and slapped a hand on his shoulder. He spun Caine round to face him, making Caine's deputies walk towards them.

'Give me a name,' Gabriel muttered.

Caine twisted away from Gabriel's grip.

'When you've helped me bring down Nyle King I'll talk.'

Caine and Gabriel locked gazes and after a few moments Gabriel shook his head.

'That price is too high.' Gabriel pointed at Caine. 'I'm leaving.'

He would have said more, but with Thorpe and Raul only a few paces away he figured arguing wouldn't gain him anything. He started to turn away, making Caine smile.

A burst of anger tightened Gabriel's chest. He swirled round and launched a round-armed punch that slammed into Caine's jaw and sent him reeling before he tipped over on to his back.

Gabriel took two long paces to stand over Caine, so Thorpe moved in to restrain him, but the marshal raised a hand, ordering him to stay back. Then he felt his jaw as he glared up at him.

'Assaulting a lawman is a serious offence,' he said. 'But don't worry. I know how we can make this right.'

Gabriel sneered. 'That's how our partnership started and I'm not making that mistake again.'

Gabriel turned away, but Caine only chuckled.

'You ought to,' Caine shouted after him. 'Have

you considered that this investigation could lead you to the man you want?'

Gabriel paused for a moment, but he shook away the thought of relenting and moved on.

'Go to hell,' he called over his shoulder.

'If I do, you'll be at my side,' Caine shouted after him. 'You're my deputy and you'll do my bidding for as long as I say you will. You don't walk away from me. You're mine!'

Caine continued to shout taunts and demands that he return, but Gabriel kept going.

In short order he mounted his horse and rode back down the gulch. It was no problem for him to avoid looking back, but it was harder for him to work out what he should do next to resolve the issue that had led to him working for Caine.

Six months ago, Gabriel's brother, Hugo, had been on the train to Lone Ridge when, a few miles out of Richland, a bandit gang had raided.

Hugo was a low-life who had spent more time breaking the law than following it, but he had also been impetuous. He'd tried his luck and jumped one of the raiders, but he'd been gunned down.

When Gabriel had got to hear about the incident, he figured that as Hugo had been his only kin and that for once he'd behaved decently, he owed it to him to help track down the raider who had

18

shot him.

Gabriel was a bounty hunter and so he had the skills to complete the task, but in this case he failed. Nobody knew who the three masked raiders were and there were so few leads that the official search for them soon died out.

Before long, Gabriel had resorted to following ever more tenuous leads and employing further dubious tactics to gather information. One day his anger at the lack of progress had got the better of him and in Richland he beat up a train engineer who wouldn't talk and who in truth probably knew nothing useful.

That was when he met US Marshal Caine. Caine was set to arrest him, but Gabriel's justification for his behaviour intrigued Caine and when he explained why, Gabriel was equally intrigued.

Caine reckoned he knew who had raided the train, but he had no proof and so he'd been waiting until the suspects stepped out of line again. Gabriel asked for the details and although Caine wouldn't discuss his suspicion, a deal had been struck.

Gabriel then tracked down an outlaw and earned his trust so that Caine could catch him in the act of committing a crime. Gabriel expected that he would then get a name, but Caine had claimed that his help had only wiped out the case against him for beating up the engineer.

An argument had erupted and Gabriel had nearly walked away, but against his better judgement he had let himself be talked into working for Caine for a second and final time.

Now that Caine had again double-crossed him, he would never let himself be talked into helping him again, but that meant his time with Caine now felt wasted as he was no further forward with his quest to find Hugo's killer. All he did know was that Caine suspected who that man was and, if Caine's final offer was to be believed, that man was connected to his current investigation.

Gabriel emerged from the gulch in a thoughtful frame of mind and rode back towards Jackson's Pass. When he reached the entrance to the pass and the trading post first came into view, he hadn't decided whether he could trust Caine's claim, but he figured that working on the basis that he had told him the truth would give him a place to start.

He moved on to the post, figuring that was as good a place as any to start his investigation. He drew up at the door and noted the horses in the corral at the side.

Several horses had been there earlier, but at the time he hadn't paid attention to how many, so in a cautious frame of mind, he moved to the door and listened.

It was quiet within and he backhanded the door open and slipped inside. The room appeared deserted and that made him flinch when he noticed that Wilson's body was no longer lying over the counter.

He moved back to the door, but a rustling sounded behind him a moment before a hand slapped down on his shoulder and hard metal jabbed into his back.

'Now why are you snooping around in here?' his assailant asked.

'I know who our mystery body is,' Deputy Edgar Newhall said when he joined Sheriff Morrison in the law office. 'It's Alvin Owens.'

'I've never heard of him,' Morrison said.

'He's a pickpocket from Richland who arrived in town a few days ago. He tried his luck in the Four Star saloon, but he was recognized and thrown out. I assume he then went to the Silver Palace saloon.'

'It's possible, but we'll probably never know for sure.'

Edgar moved on to his desk. He sat down and wondered whether to mention the matter to which he already knew the answer.

'What did Nyle say about it?' he said, figuring Morrison would expect him to ask.

21

'I didn't talk to him. I reckoned I'd wait and see what he does next.'

'I'd guess it'll be nothing, but this time that policy could work. I gather that Marshal Caine was asking about Alvin and that might spook Nyle enough to incriminate himself.'

Morrison scratched his forehead as he showed his surprise.

'The marshal was interested in Alvin Owens?'

Edgar thought for a moment and then shrugged.

'He didn't mention him by name.'

'That's what I thought. When he talked with me, he wanted to know about any thieving going on recently and about the chances of bringing Nyle to justice.'

'I'm pleased someone's worried about him,' Edgar said.

Morrison narrowed his eyes. 'What's that supposed to mean?'

Edgar hadn't meant his comment to have any meaning other than his relief that Caine was interested in Nyle, but having brought up the subject, he didn't reckon he'd have a better opportunity to mention his concern.

'These days we're giving Nyle a lot of leeway,' he said.

'We're giving him no more than we usually do.'

Morrison gave him a long look. It suggested he was

minded to deliver the lecture he'd provided when he'd deputized Edgar after his previous deputy had become disillusioned with dealing with Nyle and left town.

Edgar didn't need to hear it again as by now he was familiar with the details.

Five years ago, Lone Ridge had been a lawless hell-hole of crime and violence. Two lawmen and then a town tamer had been hired to bring order to the town, and they'd all failed.

After two years of mayhem, Nyle King had provided that order, but only because he was the most ruthless of the gunslingers that had plagued the town and he'd eliminated everyone that stood in his way. Nyle had profited from his success, but he had brought stability that had let Sheriff Morrison step in and bring respectability to the town.

Morrison and Nyle had clashed and ultimately they had defined their roles in which Nyle would look after his own interests while staying broadly within the spirit of the law, and Morrison would deal with the rest of the town.

As a result for the last three years low level crime, sanctioned by Nyle, continued in his establishments and the occasional criminal who tried to muscle in on him was run out of town. Otherwise, the town was peaceful.

'I accept Nyle has caused less trouble than the trouble he's kept under control,' Edgar said.

Morrison nodded. 'He knows my limits, and the moment he goes too far we'll be waiting for him. A few stolen items and a few people paying protection is a small price to pay for not having people shot up daily, as used to happen.'

Edgar spread his hands. 'Except recently things haven't been peaceful. We had Orson Kemp's murder three weeks ago and now Alvin's death. In both cases Nyle was probably involved.'

'Orson was a sharper who didn't care where his goods came from, so he was as little a loss to this town as Alvin was.'

'Sure, but we still had a duty to protect them.'

Morrison frowned. 'If we can prove that Nyle's behind the recent trouble, we'll take action.'

Edgar sighed as he wondered how he could continue to probe Morrison without sounding as if he was criticizing his policy for dealing with Nyle, but in the silence he heard raised voices outside. Both men looked towards the window and when the source of the commotion didn't become apparent, Edgar moved to the window and peered out.

Further down the main drag, people were streaming out of the Silver Palace saloon while looking into the building with concern. Then a gunshot pealed out.

24

'Maybe we'll get that chance sooner than you expected,' Edgar said with a smile. 'It looks like the trouble is in Nyle's saloon.'

CHAPTER 3

'Who are you and what do you want?' Gabriel said.

His assailant shoved Gabriel into the trading post.

'I'm asking the questions,' the man said. 'And I want to know what you did with Wilson.'

His loud demand encouraged a second man to emerge from a back room. When he saw that his colleague was holding Gabriel at gunpoint he drew his gun and aimed it at Gabriel.

'There are signs of a robbery back here,' the man called.

'Is that what happened?' Gabriel's assailant asked.

'I wouldn't know,' Gabriel said. 'I got here after you two did.'

'Except we saw you heading towards the pass earlier.'

Gabriel rolled his shoulders as he tried to appear unconcerned. When he'd first come to the trading post he, Lorenzo and Emmett had taken different routes and so it was possible that he was the only one these men had seen.

'I came here earlier. Wilson wasn't around so I decided to come back later.' Gabriel gestured at the back room. 'Are you saying Wilson is in trouble back there?'

'Wilson's dead and right now you're a man who keeps changing his story. I want to know why.'

Gabriel turned around with a thin smile on his lips.

'Would I have come back here if I'd killed him?'

His assailant frowned, uncertainty now in his eyes.

'Perhaps you came back to find out what else you could steal.'

'I came here to put business Wilson's way,' Gabriel said, mindful of Caine's belief about what Wilson did here. 'I sure wouldn't want no harm to come to him.'

The man looked into Gabriel's eyes and when he had returned his gaze levelly for several seconds, he nodded.

'We all wouldn't have wanted that to happen.' He holstered his gun. 'So you can understand why we're a mite twitchy.'

'I'm Forester and that's Kirkwood,' the other man called as he holstered his own gun. 'We work for Nyle

King and he sent us here to talk with Wilson. Nyle's not going to be pleased when he finds out what's happened.'

Gabriel turned to Forester. 'I'm Gabriel Flynn and maybe I can help you. I saw two men riding away from here. They were heading towards Cartwright's Gulch.'

'We'll check that out.'

'There's more. I passed a lawman, Marshal Caine. He was interested in those men so I told him where they'd gone. I guess it's unlikely that he'd be on their tail so quickly, but on the other hand they were riding fast.'

Forester frowned. 'That lawman's been lurking around town asking questions about Nyle, so we're obliged for the information.'

When the two men turned to the door, Gabriel smiled.

'In that case, I'll head to Lone Ridge now,' he said. 'I'm sure we'll run into each other again some time soon.'

When the two lawmen reached the saloon, Sheriff Morrison took the lead in heading inside. Nyle King usually had two men guarding the door, but they weren't there.

Inside, numerous customers were between them

and the bar and they had their backs to them. Edgar soon saw what had attracted their interest.

One man had slipped behind the bar and was holding a gun on the bartender while a second man stood in front of the bar with his gun thrust forward, warning the customers not to interfere.

'I don't know you two,' Morrison called, making the nearest man swirl round to face him. 'Who are you?'

The gunman gestured at himself and then at the other man.

'I'm Clyde and this is Warren.'

'And what's the reason for this?'

The customers peeled away to give Morrison a clear view of the bar and so before the gunmen had a chance to notice him, Edgar moved to a side wall. Then he started making his way towards the stairs so that he could stand to the side of the bar.

'This hasn't got nothing to do with you, lawman,' Clyde muttered. 'I want Nyle out here now or people will die.'

'If you have a problem with Nyle, bring it to me, but only after you two men lower your guns.'

'No deal. Nyle has one minute to appear.'

Clyde gestured at Warren, who thrust his gun into the bartender's side, making him straighten up and direct a beseeching look at Morrison to help him.

'I have no idea where Nyle is and I'm—'

'There's no need to speak up on my behalf,' an imperious voice stated from the top of the stairs. 'I'll deal with this.'

Everyone in the saloon turned to look at the newcomer, Nyle. He was surveying the scene with his left hand set on his hip and the other dangling beside his holster.

'You killed Orson Kemp,' Clyde stated. 'Now you'll pay for that.'

'I have no idea who killed that man, but why should you care?'

'Orson was our brother.'

Nyle gestured behind him. 'In that case, join me upstairs and we can discuss your problem.'

'You're not wriggling your way out of this. I know Forester and Kirkwood are out of town, but I don't know who is waiting for us up there. So come down here and explain yourself.'

'I have no need for additional protection in a saloon filled with friends.' Nyle gestured around the room, receiving numerous murmured comments of support. 'So the only way you're walking out of here alive is if you take my offer.'

Nyle edged his right hand towards his gun, suggesting that this course of action could be just as dangerous.

Clyde and Warren looked at each other. They both nodded and so Warren drew the bartender along behind the bar while still keeping his gun thrust into his ribs.

When he joined his brother, Clyde aimed his gun at Morrison. Then the two men walked towards the stairs.

Edgar was five paces away from the base of the stairs and since neither man was looking his way, he adopted a casual posture while keeping a hand close to his holster. Clyde was almost level with him when he looked at him for the first time, the widening of his eyes confirming he'd seen his badge.

'Stop right there,' Edgar said. 'You're both under arrest.'

Clyde started to swing his gun towards him, but that made Morrison move his hand nearer to his gun. With a snap of his wrist, Clyde turned his gun back towards Morrison.

Then Clyde darted his gaze between the two lawmen in uncertainty as to what they would do next. Edgar took advantage.

He took a long pace forward and lunged for Clyde's gun arm. Clyde jerked his gun to the side, but he'd yet to aim it at him when Edgar clamped a hand around his wrist.

He thrust Clyde's arm high while still moving on,

forcing Clyde to take a pace backwards. Then he twisted his hand, making Clyde bleat in pain and drop his gun.

Behind Clyde, Warren backed away for a pace while muttering threats, but Morrison hurried towards him. Warren was watching Edgar's attempt to subdue Clyde, so Morrison reached him before he reacted.

Warren twisted round to place the bartender between them, but that only let Morrison drag his hostage away from his clutches and bundle him aside. Then he squared up to Warren.

A backhanded swipe to the jaw knocked Warren to the side before a shove to the chest sent him toppling over on to his back. Then Morrison drew his gun and levelled it down on Warren.

'As my deputy said, you're under arrest,' he said.

Warren narrowed his eyes as he weighed up his chances. With a sigh, he opened his hand and let his gun clatter to the floor. Morrison looked at Edgar, who nodded, confirming that he had Clyde under control.

A steady hand clap sounded at the top of the stairs. Nyle made his way down into the saloon room.

'I'm grateful you intervened,' he declared with his hands held high and wide in a magnanimous gesture. 'Lone Ridge's able lawmen have done well today.'

'It was important to show that altercations can be ended without bloodshed,' Edgar said.

'You'll get no argument from me. Violence is always the last resort.'

Edgar was minded to offer a choice retort, but he knew Morrison wouldn't approve so he took Clyde to the bar and frisked him. Clyde stood stiffly, suggesting he was minded to take any opportunity that came his way to fight back and Edgar leaned towards him.

'We'll question you in the law office,' he said in a low voice. 'We'll be interested in what you have to say, and not just about this incident.'

When Clyde furrowed his brow, Edgar glanced at Nyle, making him relax and he didn't resist when Edgar turned him away from the bar.

Morrison took hold of his prisoner. Then the lawmen escorted the brothers out of the saloon.

'When you've dealt with your prisoners,' Nyle called after them, 'come back and I can show my appreciation.'

Morrison nodded while Edgar set his jaw firm, making Morrison look at him, but he didn't speak until they were outside.

'Whatever your feelings about Nyle, you'll join me,' he said.

'I sure will,' Edgar said. 'After talking with our

33

prisoners, I reckon I'll have plenty of questions to ask him.'

CHAPTER 4

When Gabriel rode into Lone Ridge he headed past the Silver Palace saloon and moved on to the next saloon, the Four Star.

The owner, Dewey Webb, greeted him with a warm smile that made Gabriel decide he'd make this place his base. He ordered a coffee and sat by the window in a position where he could watch a stretch of the main drag as he gathered a feeling for the town.

As Marshal Caine was investigating Nyle King and he had implied that someone close to him was behind his brother's death, he had resolved to learn everything he could about Nyle. As Nyle employed men who clearly knew about Wilson's activities, it was likely that other men who worked for Nyle would have dubious pasts that could include raiding trains.

It was even possible that Forester or Kirkwood

could be the man that for the last six months he'd been searching for.

He listened in on the conversations going on at the nearby tables, hoping to hear comments about Nyle, but nobody mentioned him. He'd been sitting for an hour when Sheriff Morrison and his deputy emerged from the law office and set off across the main drag.

Gabriel couldn't see what had concerned the lawmen, but when passers-by turned to watch them and customers gravitated to the door, he joined the exodus outside. When he saw what had interested everyone, he was tempted to head back inside as the lawmen were going to meet Marshal Caine.

Caine and his deputies had brought the bodies of Lorenzo and Emmett into town along with Wilson, and accompanying them were Forester and Kirkwood. The lawmen gathered around the bodies and the other men moved on.

When Forester saw Gabriel, he and Kirkwood swung their horses towards him.

'The dead men raided the Hanging Rock trading post,' Forester called. 'Marshal Caine got to them before we did.'

'At least someone got to them,' Gabriel said.

'That's what we thought.' Forester glanced at the saloon behind Gabriel. 'When you get bored with the

Four Star, make sure you visit the Silver Palace saloon. You'll be welcome there.'

Gabriel nodded and with that the two men moved on. Presently, as the gathering of onlookers grew, the lawmen disbanded.

Marshal Caine ordered Thorpe and Raul to take the bodies away while Sheriff Morrison and his deputy headed towards the Silver Palace saloon.

Gabriel turned to follow the customers back into the saloon, but he stopped when he noticed that Caine was walking towards him. He figured that anyone who knew of his claim that he'd directed Caine to Cartwright's Gulch would expect them to speak, so he waited.

'You were talking to Nyle King's men,' Caine said when he reached him.

'They were pleased that I told you where Lorenzo had gone,' Gabriel said in case the marshal hadn't already heard the story he had told Forester. 'They invited me to visit Nyle's saloon later.'

'You should do that.' Caine glanced around, confirming that nobody was near enough to overhear him. 'I need you to get close to Nyle so that we can bring him down.'

Gabriel narrowed his eyes. 'Clearly you didn't listen to what I said back in Cartwright's Gulch, so I'll say it one more time: I won't do that because I don't

37

work for you.'

Caine winked, seemingly unperturbed by Gabriel's declaration.

'And that's the story I want everyone to believe. So make sure nobody finds out the truth.'

'Marshal Caine reported that the raiders robbed Wilson Faulk's trading post,' Sheriff Morrison said when he and Edgar joined Nyle King in his office above the saloon room. 'Then they killed him.'

'That's unfortunate,' Nyle said. He tapped his fingers on his desk. 'Wilson was a decent man.'

'Marshal Caine said he had a heap of stolen property. I'll go to Jackson's Pass later to check out the scene.'

'I'm sure there'll be a good explanation for why those items were there, but either way, I hope you can return the property to its rightful owners.'

'I'll do my best.'

Nyle gestured at a decanter on his desk. When Morrison nodded, he poured three measures of whiskey.

Morrison took his whiskey, although Edgar hesitated before he picked up his glass.

Nyle smiled, suggesting he'd noticed his reluctance and then leaned back in his chair with his glass cradled against his chest. The two lawmen sat on the other side of the desk and for a while they contemplated Nyle quietly.

Nyle and Morrison sipped their drinks while Edgar moved his glass from hand to hand, staging his own protest about having to sit with Nyle by not drinking his whiskey.

Edgar assumed Morrison was saying nothing about the accusations they'd heard in the law office as he was waiting to see what Nyle offered. Sure enough, Nyle broke the silence.

'I hope you'll deal harshly with Clyde and Warren,' he said.

'That won't be possible,' Morrison said. 'When I return to the law office I'll free them, as there's little I can charge them with.'

Nyle raised an eyebrow. 'They threatened my bartender and me.'

Morrison swirled his whiskey and smiled.

'If I charged everyone who made a threat in your saloon, the jailhouse would be full.'

Nyle nodded. 'When I deal with trouble, the varmints always take heed. I trust you can assure me that when you release these men they won't trouble me again.'

'I can assure you that I'll watch them, but I can't assure you that they won't annoy you again. According to them, you shot their brother.'

39

'I did not, but I'm relieved that their accusation lets me bring up a troubling matter.' Nyle sat up straight in his chair. 'Someone is trying to ruin me and Orson's death and now Alvin's are just two unfortunate incidents in a worrying series of events.'

Morrison sipped his whiskey. 'Are you saying that someone wanted to make it look as if their deaths were your work?'

'I am. Both men have a link to me, but that isn't the whole story.' Nyle spread his hands. 'Before that, men who have worked for me for years have moved on without explanation, my business interests have been threatened, and profitable ventures haven't turned out to be as profitable as I'd hoped.'

Morrison gave a thin smile. 'I'm pleased you've made me aware of that.'

'I deal with trouble when it affects me and that is in both our interests, but I believe this affects you, too.'

Morrison nodded. 'We have an understanding about where the line is drawn between what you do and what I do, but now it would appear that you're asking for my help.'

For long moments the two men locked gazes, their measured conversation culminating in Nyle's delay in replying hinting at the importance of this moment.

'It would, and I hope you'll provide it because the trouble is escalating and if the man behind it isn't found soon, more people will die.'

'And if you get to him first, he'll regret it.' Morrison waited, but when Nyle didn't respond he gestured at Edgar. 'I'll task my deputy with the duty of finding this man.'

Nyle inclined his head and then turned to Edgar, who tipped back his hat in surprise that Morrison had allocated this duty to him. He gathered his composure with a shrug and faced Nyle.

'Rest assured that I'll find out who killed Orson and Alvin,' he said levelly.

'I'm grateful and I'm already feeling more relaxed,' Nyle said.

The two men looked at each other and when neither man said anything more, Morrison downed the last of his whiskey and stood up.

'In that case I'll leave you two to discuss the matter,' he said.

He looked at Edgar, who thanked him with a wide smile, and then headed away. When he'd closed the door, Nyle took Edgar's glass and added whiskey to it even though Edgar had yet to take even one sip.

'If I'm to help you, you'll have to be open with me,' Edgar said. 'Then, no matter who is behind this, I'll bring the guilty person to justice.'

He took the offered glass and met Nyle's eye, hinting at the double meaning.

'I can see that I'll enjoy having you work for me,' Nyle said. 'Sheriff Morrison rarely speaks his mind, but I reckon you're different and you'll tell me what you think.'

'If you want me to be as open with you as you'll be with me, I'll have no problem with that.'

'In that case, do it. Speak your mind.'

Nyle filled his glass and brought it to his lips, but he lowered it without taking a sip, seemingly waiting until Edgar had spoken.

Edgar knew he ought to be guarded with his response, but during the nine months that he'd worked for Sheriff Morrison he'd had to bite his lip more times than was healthy for him and he'd never accepted Morrison's way of dealing with Nyle. He put down the glass on the edge of the desk and folded his arms.

'You've lied, thieved, extorted and killed to become Lone Ridge's most successful businessman. Sheriff Morrison has let you get away with plenty because he reckons that helps this town. I don't agree with him. I reckon we'll be better off without you.'

Nyle took this statement without even a flicker in his calm gaze.

'And do you believe me when I say that I didn't kill Orson and Alvin?'

'I don't, but if someone really is trying to ruin you, I'll do my duty and stop him.'

Nyle nodded. 'I welcome your honesty and you can trust that I wouldn't have sought the help of the law if I was behind their deaths.'

Edgar snorted a laugh. 'That's a good answer, but then again that's the problem. Your co-operation could be a diversionary tactic.'

Nyle furrowed his brow in a show of indignation.

'I have no need of diversions. I prefer being open, so I'll offer you this: I didn't kill them. You can trust that because I have no problem in telling you that if you cross me, you'll suffer the same fate as your predecessor.'

Edgar shrugged. 'I never had the pleasure of meeting Sheriff Morrison's previous deputy Jim Albright, but I know he left town to pursue other interests. I have no desire to leave town.'

Nyle chuckled. 'That story is what everyone believes, but that's not what happened. After Jim tasked himself with taking me on, he and I had a conversation not unlike the one we're having. So I had him killed.'

Edgar stared at Nyle agog, unable to hide his shock.

'Are you saying that Jim died and yet nobody knows?'

'I am because when I deal with the people who cross me, I ensure there are no loose ends. One night Jim was taken out of town. He was made to write a letter explaining his intention to go away. Then he was killed and buried somewhere where nobody will ever find the body, a fate you'll suffer if you act on your low opinion of me.'

Edgar pointed at Nyle. 'You think you're a careful man, but you've just told me something that I can use against you.'

'I know, and that fact alone should fill you with dread. If you speak one word of it to anyone, I'll kill you and whoever you tell.' Nyle raised his glass to his lips and took a gulp of whiskey. 'I hope that clarifies the situation.'

Edgar placed a finger and thumb on either side of his own glass. He gripped the glass and then with a flick of the wrist, tipped it over.

He watched the puddle of liquor spread out across the desk. When whiskey started to drip to the floor, he looked again at Nyle.

'The situation is clear,' he said. 'Now, starting from the beginning, tell me everything that's gone wrong for you recently.'

CHAPTER 5

At sundown Gabriel left the Four Star saloon and took up a position where he could watch the Silver Palace saloon from the shadows on the other side of the main drag.

He had been watching the quiet scene for an hour when Forester and Kirkwood rode into town at a gallop. They dismounted quickly and hurried into Nyle's saloon.

These men, along with several other men, had left town earlier that day. They had ridden towards Jackson's Pass, but only two men had returned.

Gabriel considered using this moment of intrigue to take up Forester's offer and visit the saloon, but Marshal Caine had wanted him to ingratiate himself with Nyle's men. As he was no longer working for him, he enjoyed the thought of reverting to his old way of working by observing and following people of interest.

His decision was rewarded five minutes later when Forester and Kirkwood emerged from the saloon with another man. He'd never seen Nyle King before, but the newcomer fitted the description he'd been given.

The three men stopped beside the saloon and talked, suggesting they'd come outside to discuss a matter where nobody could overhear them. Their behaviour made Gabriel look around.

He noticed a man who appeared as interested in them as Gabriel was. This man was lurking outside Samuel Buckhorn's workshop, but almost as if he'd noticed that Gabriel was looking at him, he slipped away from view.

Gabriel turned back to watch the three men and presently they finished their discussion and headed to the nearest stable. They walked, Nyle leading and the other two men smiling at each other, suggesting that whatever information they had given Nyle had been received well.

The moment they went through the door, the watcher returned with two men. He pointed at the saloon and then the stable.

He received a pat on the back before he moved away while the other two men hurried on to the stable. Their haste made it look as if they wanted to meet with Nyle before he left town, but they stopped beside the door.

The two men looked at each other. Then they drew their guns before slipping inside.

For a moment they moved through full light so Gabriel was able to see their features. He placed them as being Clyde and Warren Kemp. Customers in the saloon had talked about them and he'd seen them be released from the law office a few hours ago.

With their intentions now looking suspicious, Gabriel headed across the main drag to the stable. He matched the men's behaviour in stopping beside the door where he listened.

Nyle was talking and he didn't sound concerned, so feeling that he might have misunderstood the situation, Gabriel edged sideways until he could see into the stable.

Nyle was facing him in the middle of the stable and he was explaining something to his men. He didn't appear to notice Gabriel as he turned towards his horse.

The moment he set off, Clyde and Warren emerged from the shadows at the side of the building and advanced on Forester and Kirkwood from behind. Gabriel stepped forward, but Clyde and Warren moved towards their targets quickly and before he'd managed two paces, they reached them and raised their guns above their heads.

In a co-ordinated attack, they delivered swinging blows to the backs of Forester's and Kirkwood's heads with the butts of their guns, making their victims tip over on to their fronts.

The noise made Nyle swirl round while reaching for his gun, but when he saw that Clyde and Warren had already turned their guns on him, he stopped the movement with his gun half-drawn and his body twisted at the hip.

'So you two didn't heed Sheriff Morrison's warning,' Nyle said. 'That was a mistake.'

'Quit with the threats,' Clyde said. 'Drop that gun and raise your hands. Then you'll give us the answers we want.'

Nyle firmed his jaw, seemingly weighing up his chances. He glanced at his comatose men, but then his gaze rested on Gabriel, who had stopped ten paces behind Clyde and Warren.

Nyle wouldn't know his purpose in being here and so his presence appeared to convince him that he was too heavily outnumbered to resist as he dropped his gun.

When Clyde and Warren murmured in delight and shuffled forward, Gabriel drew his gun. He levelled the weapon on the nearest man, Clyde, his action making a smile twitch at the corners of Nyle's mouth before he turned around fully to face his opponents, although he kept his hands lowered.

'You won't get no answers out of me as I don't know who killed your brother.'

'We know your reputation. Anyone who crosses you regrets it.'

'After holding a gun on me, you'll find out that my reputation is justified, but that doesn't change the fact that I only had Orson thrown out of my saloon for being rowdy.'

'I'm sure that's the only time you saw him because we know the rest of your reputation. You distance yourself from your victims, so you got someone to follow him and kill him.'

As it became clear that this confrontation was about to come to a head, Gabriel edged forward, his action making Nyle spread his hands.

'Orson was shot in the face, but men who make accusations like that deserve to get shot in the back.'

Gabriel gathered what Nyle was telling him to do, but as he hoped to resolve this situation without bloodshed, he took a pace forward, the heavy footfall making both Clyde and Warren tense up.

'Lower your weapons,' he said. 'This is over.'

For long moments his opponents glared at Nyle. Then both men swirled round, their guns arcing round to aim at Gabriel.

With no choice Gabriel blasted lead at Clyde, his shot catching him in the side and making him cry out and stumble a pace.

As Nyle dropped to his knees to sweep up his discarded gun, Gabriel swung his gun towards Warren. His opponent had enough time to fire, but as Warren was still turning and sighting his opponent, the shot flew wide.

Before Warren could aim more accurately at him, Gabriel hammered a shot low into his chest that made him double over before he dropped to the ground.

Then he turned his gun back on Clyde. By this time Nyle had his gun in hand and he joined him in aiming at Clyde, but the wounded man was struggling to hold his gun steady.

Clyde shuffled a pace towards Gabriel, but then his shoulders slumped and he keeled over to lie on his back. Nyle got up and walked over to the men where he nodded approvingly before turning to Gabriel.

'You did well,' he said. He raised an eyebrow, requesting a name.

'I'm Gabriel Flynn,' Gabriel said as he holstered his gun.

'I'm Nyle King and I'm in your debt, Gabriel Flynn.'

*

'Did anything happen while I was away?' Sheriff Morrison said when he returned to the law office after his trip to the Hanging Rock trading post.

'Clyde and Warren are dead,' Edgar said with a frown. 'Your warnings didn't make them see sense. Samuel Buckhorn is dealing with their bodies now.'

Morrison winced. 'Any link to Nyle?'

Edgar headed to the stove and poured them both coffees.

'There is, but it won't help none. They tried to bushwhack him, but this man, Gabriel Flynn, was passing by.' He handed a mug to Morrison. 'Gabriel shot them up and saved Nyle's life.'

Morrison slurped a mouthful of coffee and sighed.

'I assume you've questioned Gabriel and the situation is as it seems.'

'It was, sadly. Nyle looked relieved, while Gabriel had just arrived in town and he didn't know who he was saving.' Edgar returned to his desk and sat on a corner. 'All our problems could have been over, but Nyle got lucky.'

Morrison headed to his desk and matched Edgar's posture in sitting on a corner. He gave a slight smile.

'So that means we'll just have to bring him to justice the proper way.'

'We sure will.' Edgar returned the smile. 'And I haven't had a chance to thank you yet, but I'm grateful you've let me investigate Nyle.'

Morrison laughed. 'You might change your mind when you've dealt with him for a while.'

'I've already had a taste of his attitude.' Edgar frowned. 'It was nothing I couldn't handle.'

'I wouldn't have given you the task if I didn't think you could cope, and don't underestimate what we've achieved today. Nyle promised to deal with trouble and I gave him leeway, so asking for my help must have hurt him.'

'And now that he's asked, he can never again claim that he's in control.'

Morrison nodded, but then shook a finger at Edgar.

'That's right, but dealing with a snake like Nyle is more complex than a simple matter of right and wrong. If it was, I'd have thrown him in the jailhouse long ago. So remember that you're only investigating Nyle's allegation that someone's trying to destroy his business.'

'I've been doing that, and Nyle claimed that there have been ten incidents.'

Morrison raised an eyebrow. 'I was only aware of six.'

'So you did know more about this situation than

you've told me!' Edgar spluttered.

Morrison laughed as he considered Edgar's surprised reaction.

'A sheriff should always know more than his deputy.' Morrison sipped his coffee. 'I figured that if Nyle kept quiet about what's been happening, he was probably guilty and if he came to me he was probably innocent. I've been wondering how many setbacks it'd take.'

Edgar was pleased that Morrison's policy of waiting to see how Nyle reacted had worked, but he found he couldn't congratulate him.

'He was more forthcoming about Orson and Alvin. Orson paid him for protection and he made the same offer to Alvin.'

Morrison swirled his coffee thoughtfully and then set the mug down on his desk.

'As you're investigating trouble related to Nyle, you can add the raid on the Hanging Rock trading post to the list.'

Edgar put down his mug. 'I hadn't considered linking that to the other incidents and Nyle didn't mention it.'

'Nyle will only volunteer information when it suits him. In this case it's unlikely that the culprit, Lorenzo Moretti, was involved in recent events as he's never been seen in town before, but it's too early to rule out that the raid isn't connected.'

Edgar rubbed his jaw. 'And that's because Nyle used the post to sell on stolen items?'

Morrison narrowed his eyes. 'Be careful about how you word your accusations or you'll lose Nyle's assistance. Wilson traded in stolen goods and Nyle gave him protection for a cut of the profits.'

Edgar conceded Morrison's admonishment with a curt nod.

'If we're considering the trading post, that strengthens the links to Orson and Alvin.' Edgar stood up and walked to the box containing the stolen items that Marshal Caine had recovered from Lorenzo. 'Orson sold goods of dubious quality to Wilson, while Alvin was a pickpocket and it's likely that anything he stole would have ended up with Wilson.'

'That's some mighty fine reasoning.'

Edgar examined the money and jewellery in the box and then looked at Morrison.

'Did you find anything interesting out there to add to this pile?'

'That haul is all we have.' Morrison leaned forward and lowered his voice for emphasis. 'When I visited the post it'd been cleaned out. There's not even a speck of dust or a cobweb left.'

Edgar registered how suspicious this was with a low whistle.

'Someone wanted to make sure there was nothing incriminating left for you to find,' Edgar thought back. 'It couldn't have been Nyle as he only left his saloon when Forester and Kirkwood returned to town, but they'd been gone for a while.'

'As I told Nyle I was going there, it's likely that those two cleared out the building but taking him on will require a careful collation of evidence, so don't jump to conclusions.'

Edgar sighed as he weighed up whether this was a good moment to broach a subject that would always be hard to mention without raising Morrison's concern.

'Is that what my predecessor did?' Edgar waited, but when Morrison looked at him oddly, he shrugged. 'When you deputized me, you said that Jim Albright had been investigating Nyle, but the strain had been too much and he'd moved on.'

Morrison frowned. 'That sums up what happened. I never gave him permission to go after Nyle and he became obsessed with him, a bit like you've become. But in truth, I have no idea whether he left because of this saloon girl, Bertha Coe, or because of Marshal Caine.'

'What do you mean?'

Morrison looked aside as he appeared to think back.

'Bertha worked in the Four Star saloon and Jim doted on her. When she moved on he became depressed. Then the marshal passed through to ask about Nyle. He filled Jim's head with nonsense about how he was wasting his talents and how he shouldn't be content with being only my deputy.'

'I can't understand why anyone would think that.' Edgar smiled until Morrison returned a rueful smile. 'As Jim was interested in Nyle, it might be useful to find out what he'd learnt. Where is he now?'

'I don't know. Jim's letter made it clear that he never wanted to hear about Nyle or Lone Ridge again.'

Edgar frowned. 'So you're sure that he left town safely and that nothing bad happened to him?'

Morrison looked at him with a furrowed brow, but when Edgar returned his gaze levelly he dismissed the matter with a shrug.

'There's no reason to think otherwise.' Morrison smiled. 'And I hope that dealing with Nyle doesn't make you want to leave town like he did.'

'So do I,' Edgar said.

CHAPTER 6

'Did the lawmen accept your explanation?' Nyle asked when Gabriel rejoined him in the stable.

The bodies had now been taken away while Nyle's men were leaning back against the stable wall, nursing sore heads.

'Deputy Newhall did, although he still has to talk to Sheriff Morrison,' Gabriel said.

Nyle shrugged, as if this was a minor issue and then gestured for him to come closer.

'Edgar tells you what's on his mind, so I'm sure there'll be no repercussions.' He smiled. 'Now tell me how I can repay you.'

'I wasn't looking for payment. I'm just pleased I could help.'

'That makes me even more determined to show

my gratitude. There must be something you want: money, work. . . ?'

Marshal Caine would be pleased that Gabriel had got this close to Nyle and if he'd still been working for him, he'd have taken up his offer of work. But, mindful of his decision not to follow Caine's bidding, he turned away and rubbed his brow as if he was pondering about his response.

Then he turned back to Nyle and watched him carefully for his reaction.

'There's one thing I want, but I doubt you could help.'

Nyle laughed. 'I'm a man with some influence, so if it's a problem I can solve, I'll do it. If it isn't, I'll admit it's beyond my capabilities, so you have nothing to lose by asking.'

'In that case, six months ago my brother was killed. He was a passenger on a train heading from Richland to Lone Ridge when three bandits raided the train and shot him. I've been searching for his killer, but nobody knows anything.'

Nyle gnawed his lip as he thought about his response. Gabriel noted that he glanced at Forester and Kirkwood, although he couldn't detect whether that implied their guilt.

'I remember that raid and I recall that nobody was held responsible. I won't make any promises that I might not be able to fulfil, but I'll see what I can find out.'

'I'll be obliged for any help you can provide and I can understand how it might put you in a difficult position.'

Nyle nodded. 'I'll have to call in favours and ask questions of people who might not be prepared to answer, but I'm mindful of the fact that I'm only alive to do that because of you.'

Gabriel edged closer to Nyle and lowered his voice for emphasis.

'If it helps, I don't need to know where your information comes from and I'll deal with the killer myself. It also won't concern me if you're open with whoever you speak to and the killer learns that I'm after him.'

'It does help and having seen you in action it should concern the killer.' Nyle looked aloft for a moment and then smiled. 'I have to leave town to deal with a minor matter, but when I return I'll get you a name.'

It was past noon when Edgar headed out of Lone Ridge.

He had spent the morning trying to find people who had dealt with Orson Kemp and Alvin Owens. The stories he'd heard were varied and unhelpful.

Most people hadn't met either of them and those that had spoke of furtive men who were clearly up to no good. Nobody had seen the events that had led to their demises and Edgar hadn't got the impression that anyone was hiding anything.

In his experience, when people reported similar stories, that was because they had agreed on a version of events beforehand while vague answers were more likely to be honest recollections.

If he was to take Morrison's advice and be impartial, he could only conclude that Nyle had told the truth, that he had nothing to do with their deaths and someone was trying to implicate him.

With that in mind, he'd turned to a matter where he stood a better chance of proving Nyle had acted unlawfully even though Morrison was convinced that every scrap of evidence had been removed from the Hanging Rock trading post.

First he headed to Cartwright's Gulch and he found an area with plenty of hoofprints and stains that could be dried blood. He wasn't disappointed as he hadn't expected to find anything useful there and he was only helping himself to envisage Caine's ambush of Lorenzo Moretti.

Then he retraced the steps the raiders had taken from Jackson's Pass and when the trading post came into view, even from a distance it looked as if it had been ransacked. The door lay on the ground and shutters had been torn loose.

He tethered his horse to the corral fence and walked around the outside, confirming there was nothing of interest to see and then headed inside. As promised the interior was empty and even devoid of stock.

The other rooms were just as empty with Wilson's living quarters having been stripped of furniture and belongings. Wilson had no family, so such a determined effort to leave nothing was strange.

In Edgar's suspicious frame of mind, he could only conclude that Nyle was worried that something here could incriminate him, so he'd taken no chances and ordered his men to remove everything. As that begged the question as to where they had taken it all, he headed outside and searched for tracks.

He soon located fresh wheel ruts that headed down the pass and away from Lone Ridge. The depth of the tracks suggested it was a heavy wagon, so with the encouraging thought that something that large wouldn't be easy to hide, he mounted his horse and followed the trail.

He rode beside the tracks along the five-mile stretch of the pass and when he reached the exit, the trail veered to the west towards the long ridge that gave the town its name. He followed the trail to the base of the ridge and then rode along the bottom of the steep incline.

A mile on the tracks ended. In a pensive mood, he dismounted and confirmed that the end was an abrupt one.

He dropped to his knees and noted the soft ground had been swept around, suggesting that someone had removed the signs of the wagon's passage.

For the next half hour he scouted around, but he failed to pick up the tracks again. He stood with his hands on his hips looking at the ridge that was riddled with caves and crevices that were large enough to hide a wagon.

The sun was dipping down behind the ridge so as he still had at least an hour of daylight, he was minded to continue searching, but he recalled that Nyle had boasted about burying Jim's body somewhere where nobody would ever find it. If that was true, the wagon could be in the same type of place and he would probably need more time than he had available today.

He noted his position and then headed back to town. When he arrived in the law office, he reported his finding to the approving sheriff.

Morrison agreed with his line of thinking and promised to help him search the next day, although, as it turned out, the morning brought some fresh trouble. Overnight a thief had been at work in the Busted Flush hotel, slipping quietly into rooms and stealing valuables from several patrons.

As Nyle owned the hotel, this incident could be another attack on his business interests, so Morrison decided to investigate the robberies, leaving Edgar to head to the ridge to follow up his hunch.

With Edgar feeling that events were moving decisively, he started his search in an optimistic frame of mind, but that optimism soon died out.

He failed to find any new tracks, making it look as if the wagon had reached the ridge and then disappeared into thin air. He started by backing hunches as to likely places where a wagon or its contents could be left.

When that method failed, he searched systematically, starting from the end of the tracks and working his way along the ridge. That method failed, too.

By the time the sun was approaching the ridge, his enthusiasm for the search had gone and he reckoned that if he searched for another month, he wouldn't find anything.

Worse, he couldn't help but think that finding the wagon tracks had been too easy and that their purpose had been to lure him here and keep him occupied while the contents of the trading post were moved to a different location.

With his back bowed, he headed back to Jackson's Pass. He was still in a defeated frame of mind when he reached the trading post where he stopped and dismounted.

He looked the building over while wondering what Nyle might have been trying to hide by taking everything away.

No answer would come, but that thought was driven from his mind when he saw movement above him and near to the massive boulder known as the Hanging Rock. He reckoned a man was up there and he had been watching him before dropping down from view.

'I have no idea what you didn't want anyone to find here, Nyle,' he said to himself. 'But I reckon someone else is equally interested.'

Then he set off for the side of the pass.

CHAPTER 7

Gabriel was sitting at the window in the Four Star saloon when Marshal Caine arrived.

Using the reflection in the window, Gabriel noted that Caine glanced his way before he headed to the bar. He assumed that would be the extent of his acknowledgement of him, but when Caine had collected a whiskey he came over to his table.

'Are you enjoying your stay in Lone Ridge?' Caine asked as he sat down.

'It's a fine town,' Gabriel said. He leaned back in his chair so he could glance around without being noticed and he confirmed that nobody was close enough to hear them. 'You shouldn't be talking to me.'

'I figure that you told people you helped me, so it won't look odd that we're sitting together.' Caine shrugged. 'Either way, it'll be better to meet openly rather than risk being seen passing messages to each other in the shadows.'

'You could be right, but that's not my point.' Gabriel leaned forward in his chair. 'We no longer have a reason to talk.'

'So you're still insisting that you don't work for me despite your sterling work in ingratiating yourself into Nyle's confidence.'

'As you know, I'm doing that only because it'll get me closer to the man who killed my brother, a name that you've refused to give me.'

'And I'm glad I did that when you're doing so well.' Caine leaned forward to place his elbows on the table. 'Are you in a position yet to set a trap for Nyle?'

Gabriel stared at Caine agog, his finger rising to point at him as he chose his next words carefully. Then he thought better of saying something that would only repeat what he'd said several times before and which was unlikely to be any more effective now than it had been so far.

With a shake of the head he stood up and turned to the door. Caine snorted a laugh to himself, but Gabriel ignored him and headed outside.

He stood for a moment and decided that this was the right time to pay his first visit to the Silver Palace saloon. He didn't look back, but he was sure that

Caine would be watching him and that he'd approve of his going there.

As a result, he was in a sour frame of mind when he slipped inside and stood at the bar. Forester and Kirkwood were loitering near the door and Forester came over to join him while Kirkwood went upstairs.

'I'm pleased you've accepted our offer to visit the Silver Palace,' Forester said.

'It's taken a while, but I reckoned we were already meeting up often enough,' Gabriel said.

Forester laughed. 'If you continue to be as helpful as you have been so far, I won't complain no matter how often we meet, and you'll find the atmosphere in here a mite better than the Four Star. Marshal Caine isn't welcome in Nyle's saloon.'

Gabriel sneered, still feeling irritated by Caine's attitude.

'That's why I'm here. Caine talked to me and he's interested in Nyle.'

'You did right to tell me. Something will have to be done about that man.'

'Not unless I get to him first,' Gabriel said. 'That marshal has annoyed me just once too often.'

Forester smiled and turned aside to draw his attention to Nyle, who was coming down the stairs with Kirkwood. Nyle was sporting a concerned expression and when he reached the bar, he directed his men to leave him.

'I have an answer to your question,' Nyle said when he and Gabriel were alone.

'I'm obliged,' Gabriel said.

'You probably won't be. You may even feel that it's wrong, but I can assure you that it isn't.'

'I believe you'll be honest with me,' Gabriel said and then took a deep breath as he awaited Nyle's revelation.

Nyle nodded. 'In that case, the leader of the bandit gang that raided the train on which your brother was killed was a man who crossed your path a few days ago. It was Lorenzo Moretti.'

When Edgar was standing below the ledge on which the Hanging Rock stood, he tried to work out where he'd seen the man who had been watching him.

He identified a flat-topped rock that provided a good view of the trading post below and set off for it, but a commanding voice spoke up behind him.

'I've got a gun on you,' the man said. 'Stop there and don't turn around.'

Edgar stopped and set his feet wide apart.

'Who are you and what do you want?' he said.

'That's none of your concern. Why are you interested in the trading post?'

'The owner was killed and then the building was

cleared out. Do you know anything about either incident?'

'From the amount of riding around you've done for the last two days, I reckon you should quit asking questions and look harder.'

'So you're saying that the contents of the trading post are important.' Edgar phrased his reply as a comment to avoid annoying the man with more questions. 'I won't give up until I find them.'

'It doesn't help that you're looking in the wrong place.'

'And it doesn't help that someone who clearly knows something is being evasive.'

'You're Sheriff Morrison's deputy, but if you want to work anything out, stop following his rules and show some initiative.'

The last comment had been uttered from further away, so Edgar half-turned, hoping to glimpse the man from the corner of his eye.

'So are you working for Nyle, or are you the man Nyle reckons is trying to ruin him?'

'That was your final question. Now leave.'

Edgar risked turning his head. The man was no longer visible and so he set off for the Hanging Rock.

He tried to walk quietly, but the fellow didn't reappear and Edgar assumed he'd moved to the other side of the rock. He speeded up his approach and stepped up on to the ledge.

With the rock at his side, he peered at the rising terrain ahead, but he still couldn't see him. He listened intently and heard a crunched footfall behind him.

With a quick motion he started to turn, but he was too slow to avoid a swinging punch to the side of the head that made him stumble into the rock. Hands slapped down on his back and slammed him against the rock before hurling him aside. Edgar went spinning down on to the ledge and tumbled off it.

The steep slope was below him and he went rolling down it, his body turning over three times before he was able to jab in an elbow and still his progress. He lay for a moment gathering his senses and looked up to find that his assailant was hunkered down at the base of the Hanging Rock with his back to him.

The man pumped his arms as he engaged in an activity. Edgar couldn't tell what he was doing, but a small screech sounded.

The man grunted in irritation and threw something away. A moment later the acrid smell of burning reaching Edgar.

With a groan Edgar realized what his opponent was doing and leapt to his feet. His jarring tumble down the slope was still affecting him and he swayed before he gathered his balance.

He set off up the slope. The man moved again, and this time a flame flared, lighting the underside of the Hanging Rock.

The man hunched forward, but Edgar leapt up on to the ledge and grabbed his arm. His action stilled his opponent's arm before he could set the match to the fuse that lay at his feet.

The two men strained; the man trying to direct the match to the fuse and Edgar attempting to drag his arm away. While they struggled, Edgar was able to see that his assumption was correct.

There was a hole in the ledge beneath the Hanging Rock and dynamite had been packed into it. Edgar figured that the resulting blast would probably be strong enough to dislodge the massive boulder, so he redoubled his efforts to pull the man's arm away, but his opponent gave up on trying to direct the match.

He jerked his elbow back into Edgar's stomach, making him hunch over. Then a backhanded punch crunched into his nose; he murmured in pain and tasted blood as he fell over on to his back.

He shook himself and moved to get back up, but spluttering sounded as the fuse burst into life. The man spun round on his heel to face Edgar.

This was Edgar's first full sighting of his face and

he didn't recognize him.

'It's too late to stop it now,' the man said, 'Run!'

Edgar glanced at the fuse, judging that it would burn through in around a minute, the lively gleam in his opponent's eye confirming that they would need all of that minute to reach safety. The man turned away, but Edgar leapt to his feet, grabbed his shoulders from behind and pressed him up against the boulder.

'You're going nowhere,' he said. 'It's time for you to answer my questions.'

'Don't be a fool. We have to go and you already have all the information you need.'

'What's that supposed to—?'

Edgar didn't get to complete his question when the man squirmed in his grip, freeing an arm and then flailed wildly, clipping Edgar's damaged nose. The pain caused by the blow weakened Edgar's grip of his opponent, letting him tear himself free.

Then a firm shove in the chest rocked Edgar back on his heels. One foot landed on the edge of the hole, making him stumble and then fall off the ledge.

This time he managed to stop his movement after only one roll. He looked up at his opponent, who glanced at the hole and then turned to him with a horrified look on his face.

'Forget about me and run for your life!' he shouted.

He carried out his own suggestion and ran across the ledge, disappearing from view as he rounded the Hanging Rock. Edgar reckoned that he had the right idea in running uphill and away from both the imminent blast and the possible landslide.

Unfortunately he didn't reckon he had enough time to follow him, so instead, when he got to his feet, he headed down the slope at an angle to the Hanging Rock.

He ran with long strides, leaping over small rocks and rounding larger ones. With every stride he expected to hear a loud blast behind him, and he had covered only a dozen paces when the noise came, but it was a muffled one that shook the ground.

Edgar stopped and steadied himself before he resumed running. He covered a few more paces before he looked over his shoulder.

He hoped to see that the blast had failed to achieve what his adversary had wanted, but he had to gulp. The Hanging Rock was toppling forward while the ground and rocks around it were rolling down the slope.

Then a deep rumbling sounded and a long stretch of the pass broke away and went surging downwards in a solid wall of rocks and earth. Despite the fact that Edgar was running at an angle, he would still have to cover dozens of yards to get to a point of safety beyond the end of the ground that was moving.

Edgar started leaping in great bounds, covering as much distance as he could, but with every jump the noise behind him became louder. Then even the light level dropped as dust spread out above the advancing landslide, and the bottom of the pass was still over a hundred feet away.

CHAPTER 8

'I can understand why you thought I wouldn't believe you,' Gabriel said when he had recovered from the shock caused by Nyle's revelation.

'Naming a dead man as the culprit is a trick many might play,' Nyle said. 'I'm not like other men. I don't avoid difficult truths, especially in this case when the answer concerns me almost as much as it concerns you.'

'And that's because you knew Wilson Faulk?'

Nyle rocked his head from side to side as if he was choosing his words carefully.

'I employed Wilson for some of my business interests, just as I once employed Lorenzo, but it'd seem that Lorenzo turned against me.'

'There was talk in the Four Star saloon that someone is trying to ruin you. Do you reckon Lorenzo's action was a part of it?'

75

'I believe most things that have happened in Lone Ridge recently are a part of it, but that's my problem and not yours.' Nyle spread his hands. 'Have I honoured our agreement to your satisfaction?'

Gabriel looked aside as he pondered. He accepted that Nyle might have lied to avoid the uncomfortable truth that the culprit was someone who was alive and working for him, but despite Nyle's reputation, he trusted him more than he trusted Marshal Caine.

Caine had promised him that his brother's killer was connected to his current mission and it was not atypical behaviour for him to keep secret the fact that Lorenzo was the man he wanted. Although now that he was considering the revelation dispassionately he noted one element that didn't add up.

'I have one concern,' he said. 'Eye-witnesses claimed that three men were in the bandit gang that raided the train. Lorenzo had only one accomplice.'

'Emmett Barclay was always with Lorenzo, but they often hired additional guns for specific ventures.'

Nyle's wording had been similar to the wording Lorenzo had used when he and Emmett had invited him to join them, adding weight to Nyle's claim.

'If there was a third man, my mission hasn't ended yet. He could be the man who shot my brother.'

'He could be, but I promised you that if you had a problem I couldn't solve, I'd admit it was beyond my capabilities. This is an answer I won't be able to find for you.'

'And I promised you that I'd be obliged for any help you could provide. You've done that and it's moved my investigation forward. I'm now satisfied.'

Nyle gave a curt nod. 'Now enjoy a drink with me. After all, you don't want to spend your remaining time in town in the Four Star saloon being annoyed by Marshal Caine.'

Gabriel hadn't realized that he'd spoken so loudly when he'd grumbled about Caine earlier. He was still feeling aggrieved about the trick that had been played on him. Before accepting a whiskey he uttered a few uncomplimentary opinions about Caine that made Nyle smile.

Then he leaned back against the bar and sipped his drink while Nyle moved away to speak with his men. By the time Gabriel had emptied his glass he didn't feel any less aggrieved by Caine's behaviour, so he left the saloon.

He was determined to get answers from Caine without delay, but he saw that he would have to wait. Caine was amongst a group of men standing outside the law office.

A debate was underway in which Sheriff Morrison was quizzing Caine's deputies. He punctuated his questions with animated arm-waving while Thorpe and Raul both had hunched shoulders.

The reason for their defensive attitudes became apparent when Gabriel moved closer and saw the body lying on the ground covered by a blanket. He stopped beside the body and waited for a chance to ask for details of who had died, but then he noticed the deputy's badge pinned to the blanket.

He winced and stepped back. Presently, Morrison stepped away from Caine's deputies and shooed the on-lookers away.

While the undertaker took this as his cue to move in, Marshal Caine glanced at Gabriel, but the presence of the dead deputy had removed Gabriel's desire for an argument.

When Caine directed Thorpe and Raul to leave with him, he didn't follow them. Then, to his surprise, Morrison turned to him and bade him to come to the office.

'I only spoke with Deputy Newhall briefly,' Gabriel said when he'd followed Morrison into the law office. 'He seemed like a fair man.'

'Edgar sure was,' Morrison said.

'What happened?'

'He was at the Hanging Rock trading post when the rock finally did what everyone who has ever seen it has wondered about. It came crashing down and Edgar got caught up in the landslide. Caine's deputies heard the rumbling, but they were too late to help him.'

'So the Hanging Rock came down, your deputy was in its path, and he couldn't get away in time.' Gabriel tipped back his hat. 'That sure is a whole heap of misfortune.'

Morrison frowned. 'It is, and there's one other aspect to this. He was on an investigation.'

'Then you need to check out all the details before you deem the death to have been an accident.'

'Which brings me to my reason for speaking to you.' Morrison smiled. 'I want you to find out what happened and to complete his investigation.'

'Me?' Gabriel spluttered. When Morrison nodded, he moved to the window and watched Samuel Buckhorn take Edgar's body away, still wrapped in its blanket. 'You want me to be your new deputy?'

'I do. You're a newcomer to town so you're likely to be impartial. You helped Marshal Caine find Lorenzo Moretti and you saved Nyle King's life. I'm pleased about only one of those things, but it suggests you're fair-minded.'

For a few moments Gabriel continued to watch Samuel and then turned to Morrison.

'I accept the appointment,' he declared.

'I'm pleased. I reckon you're the right man for the job.'

Gabriel wasn't sure about that. He had accepted the role only because he reckoned it would let him learn about recent events in town and that might lead him to the third man in Lorenzo's gang.

He also welcomed the chance to annoy Caine when the marshal learnt that he had agreed to become Morrison's deputy.

'So what was the investigation that Deputy Newhall was carrying out?'

'It'd be easier if I showed you something first.' Morrison turned to the door. 'When Thorpe and Raul brought Edgar's body back I was about to check out another body.'

They headed outside and then along to the Silver Palace saloon. The body was lying behind the building, propped up against the wall.

The victim's head was angled downwards, but even without bending down to examine the body, Gabriel could see that the man had been shot in the face. Gabriel considered the scene and then turned to Morrison.

'There are scuff marks leading up to the body, so it looks as if he was killed somewhere else and then brought here, presumably as part of this ongoing campaign against Nyle.'

'I reckoned you were a man who picked up on things quickly,' Morrison said with an approving nod.

'Edgar was investigating Nyle's claim that someone is killing low-life criminals connected to him. This is the third body left behind his saloon this month and they were all shot in the face.'

'And this latest dead man has a connection to Nyle?'

Morrison nodded. 'This is Harry Fink. He recruited women to entertain customers in the Red Night, Nyle's other, less-respectable saloon in town. His demise is no great loss, other than to Nyle.'

'I was warned about that place. I assume you'd prefer me to check out what happened to Edgar before worrying about this one?'

Morrison shook his head. 'We treat everyone the same and you needed to see this before you looked into Edgar's death. Edgar was searching for a wagon that had been used to clear out the trading post. I guess he discovered something Nyle would prefer to be kept secret so he arranged for him to have an accident.'

Gabriel tipped back his hat. 'Nyle can't get away with that.'

'He can't. In the past I've given Nyle leeway on the basis that he didn't cross the line. Today he crossed that line.' Morrison pointed at Harry's body. 'While I see Nyle, learn what you can from this body and then arrange for it to be taken away. It's getting late, so tomorrow morning we'll head out to Jackson's Pass and see what happened there for ourselves.'

With that Morrison headed away. Gabriel did as he'd been told and looked the scene over, confirming that there was nothing else he could learn here beyond the facts he'd already noted. Then he moved the body away from the wall and laid it down on its back.

The disfiguring facial wound was bad enough to ensure that Samuel Buckhorn would insist on the coffin remaining closed, and that thought made Gabriel stand up straight and step away from the body. He put a hand to his brow as he thought about the reason behind that rumination.

Six months ago, an undertaker in Richland had told him that it'd be better for him if he didn't view his brother's body because his brother had been shot in the face. Just now Morrison had said that the other men who had been killed here recently had been shot in the same manner.

Gabriel whistled under his breath as he connected these facts in a way that felt logical.

'The man who's trying to ruin Nyle,' he said to himself, 'is the man who killed my brother.'

CHAPTER 9

'What did Nyle say?' Gabriel asked when Sheriff Morrison returned to the law office.

'He claimed that he knew nothing about Edgar's death,' Morrison said. 'He was equally surprised to hear about Harry Fink's demise.'

'I'd guess you don't believe him about Edgar?'

'I don't, but Nyle is too careful to make it easy to prove anything. You have a difficult task ahead.'

Gabriel nodded. 'I reckon we only have to prove he had Edgar killed. I'm inclined to believe that someone is trying to undermine him.'

'So am I, but what's convinced you?'

Gabriel looked aside as he worked out what he could tell Morrison about his recent conclusions.

Lorenzo Moretti had decided to raid the Hanging Rock trading post only after talking to someone who he had worked with before. Lorenzo and Emmett had met the informant near Richland and Gabriel hadn't seen him. Afterwards, Lorenzo had told him what their next venture would be.

Clearly Lorenzo hadn't known that the raid would be as lucrative as it had turned out to be and that suggested his informant had an ulterior motive. Gabriel now reckoned that this was the man who was trying to destroy Nyle and therefore the same man for whom he had been searching the last six months.

He didn't want to talk about his quest nor his involvement with Lorenzo as that could lead to complications he didn't want to deal with at that moment. So he settled for mentioning the other matter that he reckoned Morrison wouldn't know.

'When I saved Nyle's life I reckon I saw our mystery man,' he said.

Morrison flinched in surprise. 'You haven't mentioned that before.'

'That's because I've only just pieced things together. When Nyle left his saloon this man was watching him. Then he slipped away behind Samuel Buckhorn's workshop and returned with Clyde and Warren. He pointed out Nyle and they ambushed him.'

'Did you get a good look at him?'

Gabriel shook his head. 'No. He was too far away, but I figure that's how he operates. He slips through the shadows at night and does his work unseen, and during the day someone is giving him a place to hole up in.'

'That's how I figure he works, too. Someone is hiding him and my best guess is Dewey Webb, the owner of the Four Star saloon.'

Gabriel shrugged. 'I've talked with Dewey and he seems a decent man.'

'He is, which is why he might help someone who hates Nyle. He has rooms above the saloon for people who want to enjoy some time alone with his saloon girls or who aren't particular about where they stay.'

'I'm staying there.'

Morrison winced and then opened and closed his mouth as he struggled to find the right response.

'Then while you're there, keep a lookout for anyone acting oddly.'

Gabriel laughed at Morrison's discomfort, making him smile.

'I already have and I reckon I'm the only one who has stayed there for more than a few hours.'

Morrison patted Gabriel's back. 'I can see you'll do this job well. You're observant and you've done some fine reasoning there. I was right to take Marshal Caine's advice.'

Gabriel grimaced. 'What advice?'

'I told him I needed a new deputy and he said that you'd be ideal.'

'Is that all he said?' Gabriel snapped.

Morrison frowned. 'You don't sound pleased about getting his approval.'

Gabriel gnawed at his bottom lip, ensuring that his angry retort about Caine was left unsaid.

'I guess I don't like hearing that I'm being talked about.'

Morrison considered him, but when Gabriel didn't say anything more, he confirmed that they would meet up again tomorrow morning to check out Jackson's Pass. Gabriel left him and in a thoughtful frame of mind, he headed to the Four Star saloon.

He had intended to go straight to his room but, as he crossed the saloon room, the sight of Marshal Caine sitting in what used to be his usual place at the window made him stop. Caine smiled at him and against his better judgement, Gabriel walked up to his table.

'I hope you're enjoying being a deputy,' Caine said. He licked his lips, hinting at the double meaning as he pushed out a chair.

Gabriel folded his arms and ignored the invitation to sit down.

'Sheriff Morrison seems to be a decent man who'll

tell me everything I need to know,' he said, deciding this wasn't the right time and place to mention what Nyle had told him about Lorenzo Moretti. 'I like working for him.'

'I'm pleased. I'm sure you'll do good work for him and it'll let you learn plenty about Nyle to aid my mission.'

Gabriel shook his head. 'As I don't welcome being manipulated, I'll be doing only one of those things.'

'You're not being manipulated. You work for me and you're doing a fine job, but I can't accept my deputy going too far in the pursuit of justice. Morrison will make sure that doesn't happen.'

'And yet you didn't tell him that I'm your deputy.'

When a huge grin appeared on Caine's face, Gabriel noted his slip of the tongue. Caine chuckled, clearly relishing his retort, but in irritation with himself as much as with the marshal, Gabriel made a fist.

Caine didn't react and Gabriel accepted that despite his anger he wouldn't hit the marshal. So instead he slammed the fist down on the table.

The movement rocked the table, spilling Caine's drink and making the glass tip over and roll to the floor. For some reason, the tinkle of smashing glass only made Gabriel even more annoyed and he grabbed the end of the table and with a snarl upended it, leaving Caine still sitting on his chair.

As customers swirled around to watch them, Caine got up to face him. Before he could remonstrate with him, Dewey Webb hurried out from behind the bar and stood between the two men.

'That's enough,' he said with his hands raised to both men. 'I run a friendly saloon and I sure won't accept two lawmen slugging it out in here.'

Caine frowned and backed away for a pace while Gabriel felt his need for a confrontation leak away. He waved a dismissive hand at Caine and made his way to the stairs.

When he reached his room, he stalked back and forth until he decided that the altercation had been a long time coming. Now that it had happened and then been defused before either of them had made a fool of himself, he knew it would help to define terms between them and that from now on, he wouldn't have to deal with Caine so often.

He settled down on his bed and that conclusion let him have a good night's sleep, but in the morning his good mood soon died out. Marshal Caine and his deputies had elected to accompany Sheriff Morrison and himself to Jackson's Pass.

Caine stayed back while Morrison reported that the marshal planned to complete his investigation into Lorenzo's activities by tracking down the wagon that had been used to take away the contents of the trading post.

Gabriel accepted the news without comment and in silence, the group rode to the pass. When they first saw the scene of the landslide, they stopped to let Raul explain what he and Thorpe had seen the previous day and where they'd found Edgar's body.

Then they moved on to the base of the heap of fallen rock. The trading post hadn't been in the path of the landslide and it was intact, although several outlying fallen boulders nudged up against the walls.

'So if there was intent behind the landslide and it was to bury the trading post, it failed,' Caine said.

'You're assuming plenty,' Gabriel said. 'It's just as likely that the intent was to kill Edgar.'

'You're assuming plenty, too. We don't know yet if this landslide was deliberate.'

Gabriel gestured at the nearest boulder. 'Except if someone did kill him, clearly they wanted to make it look like an accident.'

Caine sneered. 'There are easier ways to kill a man and make it look like an accident than making rocks roll down a slope.'

Gabriel looked along the sprawling mass of boulders that filled most of the bottom of the pass for hundreds of feet beyond the trading post. His gaze alighted on Morrison who was looking at him oddly, making him accept that he had taken the first opportunity to bicker with Caine.

'You're right,' he said, resolving to try to avoid making their antipathy obvious. 'Let's see what we can find to prove what happened here.'

Morrison muttered that he agreed and while Caine and his deputies headed into the post, he and Gabriel picked out a route up the slope. Morrison led the way, directing them to a spot where the Hanging Rock had once stood.

When they were standing on the ledge, it was obvious that the boulder had started the landslide. Below this point the ground was smoother and had fewer large rocks than above.

Morrison got down on his knees and peered at the ledge. He soon located a blackened and fractured hole and Gabriel knelt on the other side of it to examine what had interested him.

'That's one question answered,' Morrison said. 'Someone set off dynamite and that started the landslide.'

'It answers one question and creates three new ones,' Gabriel said. 'Who did it? Why would that person want to destroy an empty building? And did they notice Edgar down below?'

'We won't be able to answer any of those questions here.' Morrison stood up and looked down at the trading post where Caine was slipping out through the doorway that was partially blocked by a large rock. 'I'll head back to town and see what Nyle says about this now that we know it was deliberate. You'll stay with the marshal and help him search for the wagon that was used to clear out the post.'

Gabriel winced. 'I'll be more use backing you up when you see Nyle.'

'No. Edgar was convinced that finding the contents of the trading post was important. As two of the men who have died recently are loosely connected to the items that Lorenzo took from there, I'm backing his hunch.'

'I agree they need to be found, but I doubt I can be of much use. I don't yet know the area well.'

'Neither does the marshal, although I told him where the tracks Edgar found ended.' Morrison turned and faced Gabriel. 'Is there any reason why you don't want to ride with him?'

Gabriel shrugged. 'I'd prefer not to talk about it.'

'Then is there a reason that'll stop a deputy lawman from carrying out his duties?'

Gabriel sighed. 'I guess not.'

'Then support him as you would support me. You've shown promise, but that won't count for nothing if you can't find a way to deal with whatever problem you have with Marshal Caine.'

Morrison waited until Gabriel nodded. Then they made their way back down into the pass. When they reached the bottom, Morrison passed on the details of what they'd found to Caine.

With this confirmation of what had happened here, Caine sighed.

'So someone tried to destroy an empty building,' he said.

'It's even more baffling than that,' Morrison said. 'Someone emptied out the building and then tried to destroy it, presumably fearing that they hadn't been thorough enough in removing incriminating evidence.'

'The two acts might not have been carried out by the same man. Trying to bury the building draws attention to a place you'd dismissed as no longer being of interest. So perhaps the building was emptied by someone who was worried about what was in there and the landslide was started by someone who was annoyed with how good a job the first person did.'

Morrison jutted his jaw as he thought this through and then nodded.

'If Nyle was the first man, that could mean that the second man was the man who's been trying to destroy Nyle.'

Caine grunted that he agreed and the two lawmen

92

smiled at each other until Morrison signified that he'd return to town. With a heavy heart, Gabriel watched him move away and then turned to Caine.

'I'm staying to help you,' he said.

'So nothing's changed there,' Caine said.

CHAPTER 10

Once the group had worked their way around the landslide that blocked the pass, Marshal Caine had no trouble picking up the wheel tracks left by a large wagon. Then they headed down the pass and carried on to the ridge where Edgar had searched without success.

When they reached the point where the tracks ended, Caine called a halt. The four men faced the ridge and Caine pointed out the areas where Deputy Newhall had searched, although as the deputy had passed on only sketchy details of his endeavours to Morrison, that didn't help them much.

'We don't know the area as well as Deputy Newhall did,' Caine said, 'but I reckon that can work in our favour. He searched where he reckoned someone might hide something, but we won't have any pre-conceptions. So we start here and spread out in wider circles.'

Thorpe and Raul both nodded. Gabriel knew he ought to accept Caine's sensible idea and not indulge in bickering again, but without thinking he found himself speaking up.

'That could take days with no assurance that we'll find anything,' he said.

'It could, but being methodical is what being a lawman is all about.' Caine smirked. 'But if you've got a better idea, I'm sure we'd all like to hear it.'

Caine glanced at Thorpe and Raul, making them laugh. Gabriel reckoned he deserved that retort, but having created the problem for himself, he looked around and then pointed at a low point on the ridge.

'I'd suggest that Deputy Newhall was right and that being a lawman is also about backing your instincts. I reckon we'd do better if we tried to think like the people who brought the wagon here.'

Caine looked where Gabriel was pointing and frowned.

'So you reckon they'd sweep away their tracks and then act like fools by only heading to the nearest place on the ridge?'

'It would be foolish if they were looking for some-where nearby to hide the wagon, but it's sensible if

95

they were trying to get away instead.' Gabriel gestured back towards Jackson's Pass. 'And we've not come far from Lone Ridge. I reckon they'd go further away before hiding the wagon.'

Thorpe and Raul both nodded before looking at Caine, who accepted that Gabriel had made a good point by gesturing ahead for him to lead the way.

Gabriel had only argued his case to avoid giving in to Caine, so he didn't expect his hunch to succeed, especially when Edgar had searched the nearby area, but when they approached the summit of the ridge Raul stopped. He pointed at the ground and when the others gathered round, Gabriel saw that he was indicating a wagon wheel rut in a patch of soft ground.

Thorpe and Raul both smiled at Gabriel, but Caine didn't meet his eye before they moved on. The terrain was predominately rocky so they weren't disheartened when they rode over the summit without coming across any further signs of the wagon's passage.

The only way forward would take them into a ravine so they led their horses down to ground level and searched around. Again Raul found a depression in softer ground and as Caine nodded in approval, they mounted their horses.

'I'm surprised Deputy Newhall missed these

tracks,' Caine said, speaking for them all.

'I'm the only one to find anything and I took a while,' Raul said. 'But that's to be expected. The ground is rocky so they're easy to miss.'

'Not for my eagle-eyed and resourceful deputies.'

Caine looked at each man in turn, and Gabriel decided not to make the obvious retort that he wasn't Caine's deputy. Instead, he beckoned for Caine to take the lead and when they moved on, he looked ahead with enthusiasm.

When they reached the entrance to the ravine, they scouted around and this time it was Thorpe who found wheel ruts that tracked in an unbroken line along the side of the ridge.

They followed the tracks that were now as obvious as they had been before they reached the ridge. Before long Thorpe and Raul were murmuring to each other that they, like Gabriel, thought that they would end up at the far end of Cartwright's Gulch.

Sure enough, two hours later they reached the gulch. The tracks veered into the gulch and so they rode along it on a winding path that was now leading them back towards Lone Ridge.

'Do you reckon we're being led on a chase?' Thorpe called ahead to Caine.

'Ask Gabriel,' Caine shouted over his shoulder. 'He has all the answers today.'

Gabriel didn't detect any sarcasm in his tone and so he looked around.

'There are plenty of places to hide a wagon here and I'd guess Nyle wanted it to be taken somewhere secretive, but where he could reach it easily.'

'That's a good guess.' Caine pointed ahead. 'But it doesn't explain that.'

Caine drew his horse to a halt at a point where he could see around the next bend in the gulch and waited for everyone to catch up with him. Gabriel joined the others in offering an incredulous look when he saw that a large wagon was ahead.

'So it was a chase,' he said.

'It sure looks like it, but we still have to check it out,' Caine said before beckoning for everyone to spread out.

Thorpe and Raul peeled away to ride along either side of the gulch while Gabriel stayed with Caine in the middle. They rode on at a walking pace and slowly the rest of the scene came into view.

The wagon hadn't been left in such an open position as Gabriel had first assumed. Although it was visible from their direction, it would be less obvious to anyone coming in the other direction as the wagon was set to the side of the gulch in an area where high rocks surrounded it on three sides.

Canvas covered a heaped mound at the front of

the wagon with the back section having only smaller uncovered mounds, the contents of which weren't discernible from a distance.

'It looks as if they tried to find a secure location,' Gabriel said.

'Or a place that looks secure enough to be plausible,' Caine said.

'Or they were interrupted and this was the best they could do,' Raul suggested.

Caine nodded and drew his horse to a halt. He looked at the surrounding high rocks and then beckoned for everyone to stay where they were and remain on lookout while he checked out the wagon.

Caine rode on at a slow pace and he completed a circuit of the wagon before he moved in and peered over the side. With a low whistle he tipped back his hat and then directed a thumbs up gesture at the others.

He dismounted and moved to the back of the wagon where he vaulted up over the tailboard to stand peering down at the first mound. Then he knelt down and stood up holding an old, blackened pan which he examined before tossing it aside.

He repeated the action, throwing the next item he found aside with even greater haste as he worked his way along the wagon. Raul was on the wagon side of the gulch and he called out to him.

'Anything useful in there?' he shouted.

'This looks like the contents of the trading post,' Caine said. 'But the haul doesn't look interesting and I can't see no reason why anyone would steal it, and it'll take a while to check through everything.'

'Do you need any help?'

Caine nodded and beckoned for Thorpe and Raul to join him, leaving only Gabriel on lookout.

For the next thirty minutes the three men examined the haul, their actions becoming increasingly irritated. The possibility of a fruitless end to their search also made Gabriel restless.

He moved from side to side as he tried to watch all parts of the gulch while the feeling grew that this situation was strange. He had just decided to share his misgivings with Caine when a rider galloped into view.

Gabriel was standing side-on to the gulch and at the same moment, from the corner of his eye, he saw another rider approaching from the other direction. This man was galloping past the point where they had been when Caine had first seen the wagon.

'Trap,' he murmured to himself before raising his voice. 'It's a trap!'

CHAPTER 11

Caine snapped upright to look at Gabriel. Then gunfire blasted out.

The shots were rapid and with the reports echoing, they seemed to come from all around them as they peppered the wagon, blasting splinters away from the side as well as sending up puffs of dust from the haul.

Gabriel couldn't see where the shooters had holed up, but they must have found good positions amidst the surrounding rocks and planned their attack well as the initial volley made Raul cry out and clutch his side. Then he dropped down from view on the wagon.

While drawing his gun, Caine went down on one knee beside him. He quickly came back up and shook his head at Thorpe.

Caine then hunkered down on one side of the

wagon while Thorpe took the other side. Unable to pick out any targets amongst the rocks, Gabriel drew his gun and looked to either side at the approaching riders.

These men slowed to a halt around 300 yards away and watched him with their hands on their holsters, their actions seeming to confirm they were involved in the ambush. He watched them while Caine and Thorpe peered around, the impasse being broken when a second volley of gunshots rang out.

This time the shots hammered into the side of the wagon close to Thorpe, forcing him to duck down, but that let Gabriel see the shooters for the first time. They were spread out behind a low-lying group of three boulders at the base of the high rocks.

There were four gunmen he, Caine and the deputies had never seen before.

As their opponents didn't have as commanding a position as their opening onslaught had implied, he got Thorpe's attention with a wave and then pointed. Thorpe nodded and beckoned for Caine to join him on his side of the wagon.

While they aimed at the boulders, Gabriel moved his horse towards the shooters' position. He still kept an eye on the flanking riders, who edged forward as they waited for the right moment to intervene.

As it turned out, the shooters acted first when two

men raised themselves and fired at Gabriel. The bullets whined around his head, and Caine and Thorpe returned fire, forcing them to drop down from view, but that volley encouraged the two riders to move on.

Gabriel figured he was in an open position and when the men next fired at him he might not be so lucky, so he hurried his horse on. The high rocks on either side of the wagon soon blocked his view of the riders and so he watched the line of three boulders ahead.

He didn't see their opponents, but he slowed his horse. While it was still moving, he swung down to the ground and used the momentum to help him run for the nearest cover of a boulder that was around thirty yards from the gunmen's hiding place.

He was five yards from the boulder when a gunman raised himself. The man's gun jerked round to aim towards the horse, but when he saw that Gabriel was no longer mounted up, he did a double-take before his gaze centred in on Gabriel.

In desperation, Gabriel dived to the ground and as a gunshot pealed out, he rolled into hiding and pressed his back against the rock. While Caine and Thorpe fired at the gunman, Gabriel aimed his gun towards the entrance to the area, waiting for the riders to show.

A minute passed and none of them appeared so Gabriel shuffled sideways around the boulder. When he had a clear view of the wagon he stopped and gestured, trying to gather the lawmen's attention.

Caine raised himself and gestured at the three boulders, urging Gabriel to get closer to the gunmen. Gabriel shook his head and pointed at the entrance.

Caine looked that way and with a flinch, he appeared to notice a man in a position behind Gabriel that Gabriel was unable to see. Caine fired and, bearing in mind that the riders had so far acted in a co-ordinated manner, Gabriel took aim at the other side of the entrance.

Sure enough, a man edged into view around the endmost rock at the entrance, so Gabriel hammered two quick shots at him that forced him to back away. Their attempt to fight back encouraged the other gunmen to fire at the wagon and that made Caine and Thorpe drop down from view.

Then, for the next few minutes, both sides traded gunfire. Neither side gained an advantage and with everyone pinned down in their positions, Caine again got Gabriel's attention and pointed at the boulders that the gunmen were hiding behind.

This time, Gabriel mimed shooting, encouraging him to provide covering fire. When Caine nodded, he got up on his haunches and while keeping one eye on the entrance, he edged around the boulder.

With his back against the rock, he moved sideways until the line of three boulders came into view. As there was another boulder between him and the gunmen's hiding place, he ran towards it, his head down.

Caine took that moment to start firing and he and Thorpe bombarded the gunmen's position. The gunmen stayed down and so Gabriel reached his destination without mishap.

He raised himself with his gun thrust out before him and resting on the rock, and when he could see over the boulder, two of the gunmen were only ten yards ahead of him.

They glanced his way. Then with frantic movements they scrambled away before Gabriel could loose off even a single shot.

Figuring that the gunmen would now be bunched up, he clambered up on to the top of the boulder and snaked along until he could see down the other side.

'You men tried to trap us, but we've pinned you down now,' he called during a break in Caine and Thorpe's gunfire. 'Come out and surrender.'

He didn't expect them to comply, but he kept his gun levelled on the boulders as he waited for any of them to reveal themselves. Long moments passed without reprisals and when it came, it was the two men in the entrance who hurried forward.

These men headed towards the wagon while shooting on the run, but Caine made them pay for their assault with deadly gunfire. He cut one man off before he'd covered ten paces with a shot to the stomach that made him double over and run on for several paces before he toppled over to lie face down in the dirt.

The second man reached a halfway point to the wagon before a shot sliced into his forehead, making him cry out and drop down on to his back.

'That counter-attack sure wasn't impressive,' Caine called as he turned his gun back on the boulders. 'You'll be biting the dirt, too, if you don't surrender.'

When the gunmen didn't respond, Caine gestured at Gabriel to stay where he was and for Thorpe to climb down from the wagon and move to a position on the other side of the gunmen to Gabriel.

Thorpe acted cautiously by climbing over the far side of the wagon and then working his way around the edge of the area while keeping the rocks at his back so he could scurry for cover at the first sign of trouble. When he reached a spot that was almost side-on to the gunmen and he could cover them as effectively as Gabriel was doing, he hunkered down and waited.

Presently, Gabriel heard low murmuring ahead, so he raised a hand to both lawmen, warning them that a plan was being hatched. Then, to his surprise, a gun was hurled over the boulders and landed on the ground close to the wagon.

More low murmuring sounded. Then, one at a time, three more guns were thrown aside.

'You men have been sensible,' Gabriel said. 'Now come out one at a time.'

One man rose up with his hands raised and moved to the side to stand in Thorpe's clear view. Then he beckoned for the other men to follow him, but nobody else appeared.

Gabriel judged that the first man to surrender had also been the first man to discard his gun, suggesting that the others were reluctant to follow his lead. Caine must have come to the same conclusion as he stood up and gestured for Thorpe and Gabriel to move in on the men.

'Keep coming out and this can end peacefully,' Caine called and then vaulted down from the wagon.

His gun levelled on the gunman, Caine walked forward and Thorpe stood up and walked on. Gabriel swung his legs round and slid down the other side of the boulder.

The other three men still didn't appear, so he took

a few cautious paces forward, but then gunfire pealed out, the shots echoing amongst the high rocks. None of the men behind the boulders had fired and that made both Thorpe and Caine hunch down while looking around for the source of the shooting.

Another two shots blasted out and this time Gabriel spotted the gunmen. Two men were high up on a ledge behind the wagon, presumably having kept their presence hidden until they could use the element of surprise to maximum effect.

He shouted to Caine and Thorpe while swinging his gun up towards the ledge, making both lawmen look that way. Then another volley of shots thundered and Thorpe cried out in pain with a hand pressed to his upper chest.

Gabriel took aim and he fired off a shot, but then he saw movement from the corner of his eye as one of their opponents came bustling towards him. Gabriel jerked his gun round to shoot the running man, who in self-preservation threw himself to the ground and then went barrelling along until he slammed into Gabriel's legs, knocking him into the boulder behind him.

Gabriel righted himself, but then had to contend with a second opponent who, running at the heels of the first man, crashed into him. As gunfire continued to rattle away, Gabriel pushed the new assailant away.

The man rocked back on his heels. Then, acting in unison with the other attacker, he jerked forward and swept Gabriel aside.

As the two men pushed him, Gabriel stumbled along to stand in clear space. He shook himself and then turned back, only to find that one of the men had grabbed a rock and he was swinging it round at his head.

Gabriel ducked away from the intended blow, but the rock still struck him across the temple and he went down on his knees before pitching forward on to his front.

Scrambling sounded as the men hurried away. He pressed his hands to the ground and tried to raise himself, but his arms didn't have any strength in them and instead he flopped down, smashing his face into the dirt.

Gunfire blasted out. Then silence reigned for a while.

Unintelligible shouting sounded and the speaker came closer, but the footfalls passed by him.

Gabriel again tried to move, but he couldn't work out the movements that would get him back on his feet and so he just lay there. He again heard shouting and this time it was some distance away.

Then everything was silent.

He still lay there for some time, feeling confused and weak until a twinge of pain across his forehead made him raise a hand to his brow. The hand came away damp, but on finding that he could now move, he rolled on to his side and sat up.

The gunmen weren't close by, although the wagon was still there. Then he winced when he saw the bodies of Thorpe and Caine, both men having fallen in the last places he'd seen them.

He got to his feet and for a few moments he stood groggily, the high rocks seeming to swirl around him. When their apparent movement stopped he set off at a slow pace.

He walked around the boulders and confirmed that the gunmen were no longer there and then moved on to stand over Thorpe. He'd seen him be shot in the chest and he'd been holed twice more, leaving him lying on his back.

Thorpe wasn't breathing so he moved on to Caine, who was also lying on his back with several patches of blood marring his chest. Gabriel frowned and again looked around to confirm that the gunmen had gone, but then Caine groaned.

Gabriel flinched and went on one knee beside Caine.

'Don't worry,' he said. 'I'll get you to help.'

'Too late,' Caine said. 'Nyle defeated us.'

Gabriel shook his head. 'They didn't get me. I'll make him pay for this.'

'Then do it, but do it the right way.' A pained grimace contorted Caine's face. 'Not like Jim Albright did.'

'Who's Jim Albright?' Gabriel waited, but when Caine only murmured to himself, he leaned closer to him. 'Is that the name you wouldn't give me? Is Jim the man who shot my brother and who's now trying to destroy Nyle?'

Gabriel gripped Caine's shoulder. When he didn't reply, he took both shoulders and shook them.

'Deputy . . . Deputy. . . .' Caine murmured.

'You have to tell me if that's the name I want.' Gabriel stopped shaking him. 'If it helps, I'll admit I'm still your deputy.'

'You always were.' Caine gave a weak smile. 'You want Deputy Jim Albright.'

Caine's mouth continued to move, but he didn't make any more sounds and presently his eyes glazed. Gabriel still watched him until he was sure that he wouldn't get any more out of him and then stood up.

'Now that wasn't hard to say, was it?' he said.

CHAPTER 12

When Gabriel had confirmed that the gunmen had moved on, even taking the bodies of their fallen, he gathered together the bodies of the lawmen. He laid the three men down in the back of the wagon and harnessed up two of their horses.

A throbbing headache was making him feel nauseated and unfocused and so it took him several hours before he was ready to return to Lone Ridge.

He took the most direct route to town and although he didn't see the gunmen again, he still felt pensive when he drew up outside the law office.

Using terse sentences, he explained the situation to Morrison and then did as the sheriff advised and headed inside to rest up. He washed his head wound, finding that it didn't look as severe as it felt.

With cold water and a coffee helping to revive his

senses, he was in a more contented frame of mind when Morrison returned. Morrison sat down at his desk and he scowled several times as Gabriel went through the incident in more detail.

'So you've never seen any of the gunmen before?' Morrison said when he'd finished his story.

'I haven't,' Gabriel said and then thought back. 'But I couldn't see the two men on the high ledge clearly. They could have been Forester and Kirkwood. Either way, the gunmen were so ruthless they had to be working for Nyle.'

'I agree.' Morrison rubbed his jaw. 'Except those ruthless men only stunned you.'

'They did.' Gabriel shrugged. 'I'm surprised and relieved that they didn't shoot me when I was help-less on the ground.'

Morrison frowned. 'I'm surprised, too. They shot up three lawmen while trying to protect the wagon. Then they abandoned it.'

'I reckon the wagon was only a decoy to lure us there. Once it'd served its purpose they left it, having removed anything that implicated Nyle, presuming, that is, that there was ever anything in it in the first place.'

Morrison bared his teeth with a thin smile.

'I'm pleased you mentioned the possibility of it being a trap because I agree with you. It does sound as if someone lured the marshal there.'

Gabriel rubbed his brow, feeling for the sore spot as he caught on to the reason for Morrison's sour mood.

'I didn't do that luring, if that's what you're implying.'

Morrison narrowed his eyes as he looked him over and when Gabriel met his gaze levelly, he shrugged.

'I'm not implying nothing. I'm just trying to piece together the situation and it sounds mighty odd to me that you're the only survivor of a carefully laid trap.'

Gabriel blew out his cheeks and stood up. He walked to the window, picking a position where he could look at the Silver Palace saloon.

'I can't explain it, but maybe Nyle only wanted to defeat the marshal and as I saved his life, he was grateful enough to order his men not to kill me.'

'That's possible, but we've yet to discuss why you saved his life in the first place, nor why you only remembered seeing a man show Clyde and Warren where Nyle was some time after the event or why—'

'That's enough!' Gabriel snapped, swirling round to glare at Morrison. The quick movement made him sway and he put a hand to his forehead. 'I didn't take the marshal to Cartwright's Gulch for Nyle's men to kill him.'

Morrison leaned back in his chair, calmly noting Gabriel's burst of anger.

'I'd prefer answers to my questions rather than denials. You found tracks within minutes of arriving at the ridge, despite Deputy Newhall's failure to find anything after looking for a day.'

'It was my idea to go over the ridge, but Raul found the tracks and they were easy to miss. What else have you got?'

Gabriel set his hands on his hips, defying Morrison to offer more, but that only made the sheriff relax his shoulders even more.

'Everyone's talking about the threats you made last night against Marshal Caine in the Silver Palace saloon. Then you confronted him in the Four Star saloon and it would have been worse if Dewey Webb hadn't dragged you two apart.'

Gabriel sighed and raised his hands from his hips as he tried to look less confrontational.

'I said some things I shouldn't have, but the incident in Dewey's saloon didn't amount to nothing.'

Morrison got up and joined Gabriel at the window.

'So you did threaten him and there was an incident?' he said with a low voice while looking outside.

'There was and from your viewpoint, I can see that it looks bad for me.' Gabriel took a deep breath and turned to the window. 'It all stems from the fact that

115

I haven't been truthful with you, but those lies don't include my having helped Nyle kill the marshal.'

Morrison breathed deeply through his nostrils.

'Go on.'

'I was Marshal Caine's deputy, except we kept that a secret because I infiltrated outlaw gangs like Lorenzo Moretti's for him.'

Morrison considered for a moment and then nodded.

'I guess that makes sense.'

'Except I only helped him because he promised to give me the name of the man who shot my brother, Hugo Flynn. I started to believe he'd never help me and so we argued, but at the last he gave me a name. I reckon that man was his former deputy and he's the man who's trying to ruin Nyle.'

Morrison tipped back his hat. 'That's one hell of a story. Who is he?'

'Deputy Jim Albright.'

'Jim Albright wasn't Caine's deputy!' Morrison spluttered, raising his voice for the first time. 'He was my deputy. He left town nine months ago.'

Gabriel winced, but then shrugged. 'My brother was shot six months ago.'

The two men faced each other and Morrison shook his head.

'That doesn't mean anything. I knew Jim well.

116

Until he got it into his head to take on Nyle, he was a calm man who spent more time mooning over this saloon girl than he did patrolling the town.'

'That sounds like the sort of man who could be trying to undermine Nyle.'

Morrison frowned and looked aloft for a moment.

'Edgar also asked about Jim,' he mused. 'He sounded as if he was worried that he'd died and I assume he thought that Nyle had killed him.'

'In a way Jim did die. He's become someone other than the man you once knew.'

'I'm not convinced about that, but I'll keep an open mind.' Morrison pointed at him. 'So is that everything you need to tell me about your relationship with Nyle King and Marshal Caine?'

Gabriel decided not to mention Nyle's information about his brother's killer as at best it contradicted Caine's statement and at worst, it meant that Jim had joined a bandit gang, a suggestion that would probably make Morrison even less inclined to believe him.

'It is. There's nothing more.'

'Then I'll believe you.' Morrison waited until Gabriel breathed a sigh of relief and then waggled his finger. 'But if even one element of that story turns out to be wrong, it'll destroy your entire explanation and I will arrest you on suspicion of being involved in

Caine's death.'

Gabriel firmed his jaw as he met Morrison's stern gaze.

'I accept that, and I guess you'll only fully trust me when we've found Jim or whoever is behind this.'

'On that we can agree.'

Then both men turned back to the window to look at the Silver Palace saloon.

'Do you trust me enough to let me question Nyle about this?' Gabriel asked after a while.

'I do. Nyle has been in his saloon all afternoon. Forester and Kirkwood are on guard at the door now, but they weren't in town earlier.'

Morrison directed a knowing look at Gabriel and then gestured for him to leave. Gabriel smiled, but he took his time in walking outside as the tense conversation had caused his head to throb again.

Forester and Kirkwood looked his way, so to keep them waiting he embarked on a stroll around town. When he at last ended up at the door of the Silver Palace saloon, the cool breeze had soothed his headache, although he felt no less angry about recent events.

Forester smiled and stepped aside to let him enter.

'I'm pleased you've returned,' he said. 'Morrison's deputy will always be welcome here.'

'Nyle repaid his debt to me, so there's no need to

grant me any special favours.' Gabriel set himself between the two men. 'I sure won't hand out any special treatment to you two.'

Gabriel waited until both men bristled at the comment and then moved on into the saloon. Nyle was holding court in the corner of the saloon room to several people, but when his men followed Gabriel inside, he broke off from his conversation to watch him approach.

'How may I help you?' Nyle called.

Gabriel said nothing until he was standing before Nyle's table.

'I'm sure you've heard that several gunmen ambushed and killed Marshal Caine in Cartwright's Gulch, but luckily I escaped alive.'

Nyle gave a curt nod. 'That gunfight was a most unfortunate occurrence, but we must be thankful that you survived, Gabriel.'

'That's Deputy Flynn to you.'

Gabriel narrowed his eyes and when Forester and Kirkwood stood on either side of him, Nyle appeared to catch on to the fact that he was about to voice an accusation. He raised a hand and shooed away his entourage, along with Forester and Kirkwood.

'Leave us,' he said. 'I have matters to discuss with Deputy Flynn.'

Without comment everyone moved away. Nyle

then signified that Gabriel should sit down.

Gabriel considered whether to comply with Nyle's instruction and then with a shrug, he sat on the opposite side of the table to him.

'I told you that I was satisfied with the answer you gave me and that you're no longer in my debt, so why did you leave me alive?'

'That's a direct question. You're not even wasting time accusing me of being behind the incident.' Nyle smiled. 'I can see that I'll enjoy working with you as much as I enjoyed working with Deputy Newhall.'

'Right up until the moment you had him killed.'

Nyle shook his head. 'I didn't do that. He promised to find the man who's trying to destroy me and I believed he'd succeed.'

'Does that mean you believe I'll succeed?'

'I do, as you'll now be sufficiently motivated to find this man.'

Gabriel frowned. 'Because you reckon I'll be grateful that when you had Forester and Kirkwood shoot up the marshal they left me alive?'

'No. It's the opposite.' Nyle licked his lips and leaned forward. 'I told them that unless you gave them no choice, they should avoid killing you because someone had to take the blame for the gunfight.'

Gabriel glanced away. 'Nobody will believe I was

behind that.'

Nyle chuckled and leaned back in his chair.

'You wouldn't make a good poker player. I can see you've already worked out that this situation looks bad for you, and it can get worse. Witnesses can be found to fill in the gaps in the story of what happened out there.'

'And what is that story?' Gabriel snarled.

Nyle tapped his fingertips together as he delayed replying so that, presumably, he could enjoy Gabriel's discomfort for a while longer.

'You hired guns and then directed the marshal on a mission to find a wagonload of worthless items, but your real intent was to lead him into a trap. Then you walked away and the marshal didn't.'

'I can answer any lies that you may level against me.'

Nyle met Gabriel's eye and when Gabriel glared back at him, he dismissed the matter with a wave of his hand.

'Don't risk it when you only have to complete the mission Deputy Newhall started. Find the man I want before there are any more incidents.' Nyle narrowed his eyes. 'But if anything else happens to any of my business interests, I'll find enough evidence against you to ensure Morrison arrests you.'

CHAPTER 13

'You must have started early,' Gabriel said when he found Morrison behind the stable the following morning.

Morrison pointed inside the building at the strewn belongings, crates and sacks that had been on the wagon Gabriel had brought back to town.

'I had to check the haul you found,' he said. 'I didn't find anything of interest, which proves it must have been a decoy.'

Gabriel headed into the stable and wended a path between the heaps of items, confirming that none of them looked significant. He came out shaking his head.

'So you're saying that Nyle made it look as if something important was in the trading post by clearing it out, hiding the stolen haul, and then trying to bury the building in a landslide, except there wasn't?'

'I guess I am.'

Gabriel looked at the scattered items as he pondered and then smiled.

'Now that I'm no longer arguing with Marshal Caine, I have to admit he had good instincts. As he probably would have said, there are easier ways to kill a man than making a trail and hoping he'll follow it, and as he did say, it doesn't follow that the man who emptied the post started the landslide.'

Morrison nodded. 'Caine also reckoned that if the intent was to bury the post, it failed. So the landslide being to the side of the post could have been deliberate and the real intent was to only draw attention to it.'

Gabriel raised a finger. 'Which means that the building is important, not the contents.'

Morrison tipped back his hat as he considered this point.

'Everything keeps coming back to the post. Orson Kemp sold items to Wilson Faulk there, Alvin Owens would have passed on stolen goods there if he'd got the chance, and Lorenzo Moretti raided the place. It's only Harry Fink's death that doesn't link to it.'

'Then we haven't got the full picture yet, but maybe we'll find the rest of the answers we need at the post.'

'I searched that place and Edgar was probably killed because of his interest in it.' Morrison thought for a moment and then smiled. 'But it won't do no harm to go there again.'

With that, the two lawmen headed into the stable. In short order they mounted up and headed out of town.

They'd been riding for thirty minutes when Gabriel moved in closer to Morrison.

'I assume you aren't still concerned about my possible guilt?' he asked.

'I'm prepared to believe your story until proved otherwise and I heard about your confrontation with Nyle yesterday. Nyle looked concerned enough to suggest you weren't acting on his instructions.'

'I didn't know you knew about what goes on in his saloon.'

'A sheriff should always know more than his deputy does.' Morrison chuckled, but then hardened his expression. 'But the one fact you need to know is that my deputy and a US marshal have been killed and I won't rest until I find out who killed them. So as Nyle is able to explain his activities, we just need to poke a hole in his story. Then we can arrest him.'

Gabriel nodded, after which they rode on to Jackson's Pass. They stopped some distance from the landslide to give the rocks a cursory examination before they moved on to the trading post.

'As you know more than I do, where do you want to start?' Gabriel asked when they'd dismounted.

'I don't know, but as you've not searched the place before, perhaps you should lead.'

'I came here when I was with Lorenzo.' Gabriel thought back. 'Wilson kept his valuable items in a chest in a back room, and it didn't take much persuasion for him to lead us there.'

'He was probably confident that Nyle would reclaim them, but it's also possible he was less concerned about you finding the chest than he was about you finding something else.'

Gabriel nodded and so they walked on to the post and through the main room to the back room where Lorenzo had divested Wilson of his property. The area was as empty as Morrison had promised it would be so Gabriel tapped the walls, searching for signs of anything having been hidden behind them, but the walls were intact and they sounded solid.

He dropped to his knees and tapped the wooden floor, which encouraged Morrison to stomp around. The floor was robust and offered no changes in sound as they moved around, so they investigated the main room, with the same unpromising result.

Morrison then headed into Wilson's living quarters, leaving Gabriel standing in the middle of the post with his hands on his hips, wondering what they could have missed. He cast his mind back to the raid and he couldn't recall anything useful, but then he considered his other time here with Forester and Kirkwood.

His arrival had concerned them and they'd moved Wilson's body away from the counter. Their actions might have been innocent, so with no great expectation that he'd find anything, he walked over to the counter.

The counter stretched across most of the longest side of the room and it had a solid wooden top blocked in on all sides with short planks. He tapped the top and sides while walking back and forth, proving that an empty space was inside, and so he called for Morrison.

When Morrison returned, he pointed out what had interested him and then sought a way to remove the sides, but the sheriff used a more direct approach and kicked one end of the counter. At first the wood resisted, but when Gabriel joined him in kicking, it soon splintered and fell away.

Both men dropped down to see what they had uncovered. Through gaps in the wood, enough light filtered beneath the counter to reveal an open space around twenty feet long and four feet wide.

Nothing had been stored there, but, unlike the

rest of the post, the ground hadn't been boarded over.

'It looks like we need to start digging,' Gabriel said.

'I'll dig,' Morrison said. 'You get this thing moved away.'

Morrison rooted around through the lengths of wood they'd broken away and selected a plank with a pointed end. He started plunging it into the hard surface while Gabriel worked on dismantling the rest of the counter.

By the time he'd pulled away the top and kicked down the rest of the sides, Morrison had gouged out several holes, each around a foot deep, but he'd stopped working and he was looking at Gabriel as he waited for him to finish his task.

'Tired already?' Gabriel asked, but then he noticed Morrison's sombre expression and he moved closer.

When he could see down into the most recent hole Morrison had created, he gave his own sombre expression. Morrison had uncovered a human foot.

'I'd guess this is what Nyle didn't want us to find,' Morrison said.

Gabriel looked along the length of bare ground that had been exposed.

'Nyle's men would have had enough time to

remove one body, so I'd guess this isn't the only person buried here.'

With that gloomy thought they got to work.

The next two hours was a traumatic time for both men as Gabriel's theory proved to be correct. Bodies had been buried along the length of the counter.

The first body Morrison had uncovered looked to be the most recent, perhaps being there for only a few months, while the others had been buried for years. When they stood back they had located six people.

'This is bad,' Morrison said, speaking for them both.

'Do you know who these people are?' Gabriel asked.

Morrison shrugged. 'Plenty of people have crossed Nyle and most of them reckoned it'd be healthier for them to leave town. I'd guess they might not have always succeeded.'

'You're sure that they're Nyle's work?'

Morrison moved closer to one body. 'It'll take time to prove it, but the first one we dug up suggests that's what we'll conclude. It's the only person I recognize.'

Gabriel stood beside Morrison. Time and decay had ensured that little was left of the bodies' features, but the first body was wearing a dress and was the only woman they'd uncovered.

'Who is she?'

'Bertha Coe, a saloon girl from the Four Star saloon, often wore that dress.' Morrison directed a significant look at Gabriel. 'Jim Albright mooned over her and he left town after she, apparently, moved on.'

The first piece of tangible evidence that Jim was behind recent events made Gabriel whistle under his breath.

'It would seem that she didn't get the chance.'

Morrison nodded. 'Harry Fink tried to get her to work for Nyle at the Red Night saloon. She wasn't interested and nobody makes the mistake of crossing Nyle.'

'It might also explain why Harry was killed. Perhaps Jim hasn't just been killing random people who were connected to Nyle. He could have been killing the people who were connected to what happened to her.'

Morrison went on one knee and peered at the body of Bertha closely before standing up.

'She was shot in the face.' He sighed. 'So Nyle might have already worked out some of what's been going on.'

Gabriel sighed. 'This discovery confirms who is behind everything, including Deputy Newhall's death, but I'm not sure that Nyle knows the identity of the man who's after him, and I still can't see how my brother fits in to this.'

Morrison considered for a moment and then tipped back his hat.

'That's a concern for another day. Now we just have to prove that Nyle killed these people.'

Gabriel nodded, but then a commanding voice spoke up from behind them.

'So you're not keeping an open mind, then.'

Both men swirled round to find that while they'd been concentrating on the bodies, Nyle had sneaked into the trading post.

Nyle was standing a pace in from the doorway. Forester and Kirkwood were flanking him, their guns aimed at the lawmen.

'Your presence here proves your guilt,' Morrison said.

'I guess it does,' Nyle said. He glanced at the line of bodies. 'I should have known you'd never stop picking away at this.'

'And if you hadn't have done the same thing, I'd never have become interested in this place. Then again I always knew that one day you'd make a mistake.'

'The guns aimed at you would suggest yours is the biggest mistake.' Nyle chuckled. 'After all, I've already dealt with one inquisitive lawman this week.'

Nyle turned to Kirkwood with a hand rising, presumably as he prepared to give him an order, making Morrison twitch his hand towards his holster, and so Gabriel spoke up.

'I promised you that I'd find the man who's trying to destroy you, Nyle,' he said, hoping that Nyle had arrived too late to hear them identify Jim as the culprit. 'If you kill us you'll never get that name, until it's too late.'

Nyle turned back to Gabriel. 'You've had enough time and enough leeway to do that, although I don't intend to kill you. Again, someone has to take the blame for what's going to happen, and who better than the man who lured Marshal Caine to his death?'

Gabriel snorted. 'Nobody will believe I've been involved in the death of yet another lawman.'

'We shall test that belief.' Nyle pointed at Kirkwood and waved Forester on. 'Now, kill Morrison and secure Gabriel.'

CHAPTER 14

Kirkwood firmed his gun arm and Forester took a pace towards Gabriel, but Gabriel figured that he could use Nyle's desire to keep him alive. So he stood in front of Morrison, his action making Kirkwood move to the side to try to see around him.

Gabriel drew his own gun and swung it towards Nyle, but Nyle stepped back through the doorway and disappeared from view.

'End this now,' Nyle shouted from outside.

His demand made Morrison stand up close to Gabriel's back.

'Back away,' Morrison whispered.

Gabriel nodded and while still shielding Morrison, he stepped away from the two gunmen. They tracked backwards around the dismantled counter and then towards the door to the back room.

Nyle's men followed them, their eager grins suggesting they were biding their time until the lawmen made a mistake. As both lawmen knew where the debris from the counter was lying, they reached the doorway without mishap.

While Morrison stepped away from Gabriel and into the back room, Gabriel stayed in the doorway.

'Don't come no closer,' he said.

'We'll do whatever you say, Deputy Flynn,' Forester said with a smirk.

Both gunmen stopped beside the line of bodies, so Gabriel looked over his shoulder.

Morrison had moved to the outside door. He peered past the large rock that partially blocked the doorway and then beckoned for Gabriel to join him in fleeing.

'Step through this door and it'll be the last thing you do,' Gabriel said, glaring at the gunmen.

He backed away until he was halfway across the room. Then he hurried on to join Morrison, who led the way as they scampered outside.

Morrison managed only two paces before gunfire rattled, the rapid volley coming from behind the large boulders that had rolled down to the bottom of the pass. Lead hammered into the rock and the door frame, forcing Morrison to duck and then scramble back inside.

'Either Nyle can fire fast or more people are outside,' Morrison said when he had pressed his back to the wall.

Gabriel winced. 'Nyle gave the order to end this, but I guess that shooting means he wasn't just talking to the men inside.'

Gabriel turned to the other doorway as he accepted that Kirkwood and Forester hadn't been concerned about them escaping as they knew that they were now trapped.

'Are you folks getting settled in there?' Forester called from the other room, confirming Gabriel's theory.

When Kirkwood laughed, Gabriel snarled and in irritation loosed off a shot through the open doorway. Then he stood on the other side of the outside door to Morrison.

'You've made a big mistake by showing your hand,' Morrison called through the door.

'I don't reckon so,' Nyle shouted. 'If my men could defeat Marshal Caine, you won't do no better.'

'Except they lured him to a remote area to launch their ambush. This place is closer to Lone Ridge and before long someone will hear the shooting, and they won't come to your aid.'

Nyle didn't reply to this taunt, but scuffling foot-falls sounded as at least one man moved from the boulders to the side of the post.

Gabriel aimed at the internal doorway, leaving Morrison to concentrate on events outside. Long moments passed in silence and then shuffling sounded in the main room.

'They're coming for us on the inside,' he whispered a moment before two men Gabriel recognized from the ambush in Cartwright's Gulch hurried through the doorway, keeping low.

The men fired on the run, aiming towards the doorway, their shots hammering into the wood beside Morrison. Thankfully, Gabriel's warning had alerted Morrison and he slammed lead into the right-hand man's chest, dropping him.

The left-hand man managed a second gunshot that again hit the wall, but by then Gabriel had him in his sights and he sliced a high shot into the man's neck that made him fall over backwards.

Forester and Kirkwood edged through the doorway, but when they saw the fate of their colleagues, they jerked back out of sight.

'That wasn't impressive,' Morrison taunted. 'You should surrender now before you get what they got.'

Forester uttered an oath and a murmured debate ensued. The result of the discussion became clear when receding footfalls sounded across the main room.

'I reckon that six hired guns survived the ambush in Cartwright's Gulch,' Gabriel said.

'That means we're still facing four gunmen and Nyle.' Morrison glanced outside. 'Their next move will be better than their first effort. We need to act before they put that plan into operation.'

Gabriel nodded and they hurried across the room and stood on either side of the internal doorway. They didn't know whether the main room was still occupied, so both men slipped their guns through the doorway.

They sprayed gunfire around the room and then darted through the doorway. With quick movements, they separated and placed their backs to the wall.

Gabriel's side of the room was deserted, but Morrison turned his gun on a heap of wood that they'd created while dismantling the counter. Gabriel aimed at the wood and moved sideways while watching for the gunman that Morrison believed was there.

He'd covered three paces when a second pile of wood drew his attention. It looked too small to hide someone, but it was also in front of one of the holes they'd dug when they'd searched for bodies.

He swung his gun towards that pile and stepped forward, an act that made a gunman dart up to confront him. At the same moment, a second gunman rose up from behind the other pile and fired a wild gunshot at Morrison.

Morrison was ready for the onslaught and he hammered lead into the gunman's chest while Gabriel dispatched his opponent with a deadly shot to the forehead that made the man drop back down from view.

Gabriel hurried on and peered over the wood to confirm that only one man was hiding there and that he was lying still while Morrison did the same with his opponent on the other side of the room.

When Morrison nodded with approval, both men reloaded. Then Morrison covered the outside door and Gabriel aimed at the internal doorway while keeping an eye on the third door that led to Wilson's quarters.

This door was closed, but Gabriel recalled that before the ambush the door had been open.

He got Morrison's attention with a gesture. Morrison winked and then fired two quick shots into the centre of the door.

Wood splintered accompanied by the sound of Forester crying out. Then a thud sounded.

With the feeling hitting him for the first time that they might prevail, Gabriel ran across the room and kicked the door. The door flew open to reveal Kirkwood, but the door collided with Forester's body and rebounded, striking Gabriel's shoulder and making him stumble.

His sudden movement saved him from Kirkwood's gunshot that winged past his right sleeve and thudded into the wall. While still struggling to right himself he returned fire.

Then, from the main room, Morrison pounded lead through the doorway. One of the shots found its target, making Kirkwood stand up straight while clutching his side.

Gabriel blasted two gunshots into Kirkwood's chest, making him drop to his knees and keel over. While Gabriel checked that Forester was dead, Morrison headed to the window, the only other way out of the room.

Then, with gestures alone, Morrison outlined his plan to take the fight to Nyle. Gabriel nodded and leaned out of the window.

He confirmed that this side of the post looked down the pass and away from the landslide. As the last time they had heard Nyle he had been on the other side of the building, they clambered up on to the sill and dropped down outside.

They pressed their backs to the wall. Then they separated and moved to the opposite corners of the building.

Morrison slipped around the corner and when

several seconds had passed silently, Gabriel glanced around his corner at the tumble of boulders beyond the far end of the building.

Nyle wasn't visible, so he shuffled around the corner and along the wall. He passed the back exit and moved on to reach the far corner without incident.

When Gabriel peered around the corner, Morrison had already reached the back of the building. Morrison pointed at a massive boulder ahead.

Gabriel judged that this was the Hanging Rock and, as its journey to the bottom of the pass had left it intact, it dominated the other rocks strewn nearby. Morrison moved towards it with cautious steps, suggesting that he was backing a hunch that Nyle's ego would make him pick the largest rock as cover.

Gabriel moved on while looking for other places where Nyle could be hiding, but Nyle raised his head and peered down at them from the top of the boulder.

Nyle aimed his gun at Gabriel, so Gabriel leapt to the side and when his opponent fired, the gunshot tore into the ground inches from his heels.

Then he scrambled back and around the corner of the post, coming to a halt on his knees. He shook himself and then moved forward to face the boulder.

Nyle had dropped down from view while Morrison had found cover behind an angular boulder to the side of the Hanging Rock.

'So you two survived,' Nyle called.

'It wasn't hard,' Morrison shouted. 'Your men only knew how to win fights when their targets were out in the open.'

Nyle laughed. 'In that case this will be an easy fight. I have an ideal position and you're both pinned down below me.'

'I prefer to think that you're trapped up there and we just have to wait until help comes.'

'There's no assurance that help will come, and if it does, on whose side that help will be.'

Morrison didn't retort, suggesting Nyle had won that war of words and so Gabriel decided to try his own taunts.

'With all the bodies in there, this situation has become messy,' he shouted. 'I assume those shots you took at me mean you no longer plan to let me live to take the blame for this.'

'I don't need you alive to make that story believable,' Nyle called. 'Whoever walks away from this is the only one who'll get to tell their side of the story.'

'Even if that man is you, you won't enjoy your victory for long. Someone is watching your every move and he won't rest until you've been destroyed.

140

Now that I know who he is, your days are numbered.'

'The line of dead men in there say that this man won't do no better.' Nyle snorted a laugh of bravado. 'And you'd never have found the other bodies buried in my other secret places.'

'You're not very observant, Nyle. It's not just dead men that were buried in the post.'

'What do you mean?'

Nyle had raised his voice and he also rose up so that the tip of his hat became visible, showing that he had moved several feet closer to Gabriel.

'There are five dead men and a dead woman buried—'

'I didn't have no woman killed,' Nyle roared and then raised himself to shoot down at Gabriel.

He had yet to fire when Morrison blasted lead at him, his shot catching Nyle in the side and making him drop down on to the rounded edge. For a moment Nyle teetered as he scrambled for purchase on the smooth rock before he lost his battle to stay on the top and fell.

He slammed down to the ground in a cloud of dust and rolled on for several yards until he came to rest ten yards to Morrison's side. Both lawmen levelled their guns on Nyle as he lay on his back groaning.

Then, with a wince of effort, Nyle twisted round to

lie on his chest. He rolled a shoulder and forced himself up on to his knees.

'I reckon a court can decide whether you had anything to do with her death,' Morrison said. 'Now raise those hands.'

'I never harmed no woman.' With his gun held slackly in his grip, Nyle raised his head to glare at Morrison and Gabriel in turn. 'Who is she?'

'Bertha Coe from the Four Star saloon, the woman Jim Albright mooned after, and her death has caused all your problems.'

Nyle raised his free hand to finger his wounded side and smiled.

'So you reckon that Jim is taking revenge against me, do you?'

'Sure.'

'Then you got it wrong, lawmen. Jim was all torn up about her and he never accepted that I didn't kill her, so I had him killed.'

'Wrong. Jim's alive. Whoever you hired didn't—'

'Be quiet!' Nyle roared, anger flaring his eyes.

He pointed at Morrison, but his action had been only a distraction as he then jerked up his gun arm to shoot at the sheriff. Nyle's arm was still moving when Gabriel planted a bullet high in his chest, making him arch his back.

Nyle knelt there looking at the sky. Then he

toppled over to lie on his side where he again tried to raise his gun arm, but this time he failed and his head flopped down to lie in the dirt.

CHAPTER 15

'Do you believe what Nyle said?' Gabriel asked when he and Morrison had confirmed that Nyle was dead.

Morrison jutted his jaw as he headed back to the post.

'In my experience even men like Nyle don't lie at the end,' he said. 'And he was clearly so surprised to hear that Bertha is buried in there that he acted recklessly.'

Gabriel joined Morrison in walking away from the body.

'I guess he was.' Gabriel shrugged. 'So it was ironic that he got away with numerous crimes and then died as a result of a crime he didn't commit.'

'Don't be so sure of that. When we've identified the rest of the bodies we'll piece together everything he did, but the question on my mind is whether we got it wrong.' Morrison stopped in the doorway and

144

turned to Gabriel. 'Was Nyle right that the man who was after him wasn't Jim?'

'Nyle got others to kill on his behalf, so someone could have failed to complete his task and Jim survived, but with that man's mission over, it's likely that the law will never know for sure.'

Morrison shook his head. 'As that man probably killed Edgar, I won't rest until I have an answer, and I assume you won't rest until you get to the truth either?'

'You assume right.'

Morrison sighed as he looked at the line of bodies in the post. Then he directed Gabriel to help him gather them together.

Wilson had a rickety old wagon in the corral, but it was strong enough to cope with the weight of the dead gunmen along with the bodies they'd dug up, and within the hour they were heading back to town.

The cargo would ensure that their arrival would generate interest, both welcome and not, but Morrison delayed that potential problem by stopping outside town and directing Gabriel to move on alone and fetch the undertaker.

Another hour later, the bodies were in Samuel's workshop, and all without anyone noticing. Then both men headed to the law office where Morrison and Gabriel stood beside the door, looking at the

Silver Palace saloon.

'Even with our precautions, word will get out about Nyle's demise,' Morrison said. 'We need to be ready for trouble when it does.'

'Where do you reckon it'll come from?' Gabriel asked.

'Nyle kept a lid on trouble so it could boil over from anywhere and everywhere, and that's before we consider whether he has other hired guns in town.'

Gabriel tipped back his hat as he thought about the problems ahead of them.

'Then there's the matter of who really killed Bertha.'

'Nyle could be innocent of that, but either way I reckon that over the next few days that matter could be the least of our problems.' Morrison pointed across the main drag. 'You patrol the other side of town and I'll take this side. When the rumours start spreading, see what people think about Nyle's death.'

Morrison had chosen for himself the side that included the Silver Palace saloon, so Gabriel wished him well and set off. He moved to the end of town and started a slow patrol.

He didn't hear anybody discussing Nyle, so when he reached the Four Star saloon, he headed inside. His assumption that most of the town gossip spread from there was proved correct when Dewey Webb hailed him the moment he walked through the door.

'Is it true?' he called.

Gabriel kept quiet as he headed to the bar and then looked around the saloon room, noting that in the late afternoon he was Dewey's only customer.

'Is what true?' he said cautiously.

Dewey leaned over the bar and also looked around before lowering his voice, as if he were speaking in confidence.

'People are saying that they heard a shoot-out in Jackson's Pass, Nyle King's not in town, and Samuel Buckhorn has closed his workshop door.'

Gabriel leaned on the bar to Dewey's side and lowered his voice.

'I can see why people would connect that information and reach an interesting conclusion.'

Dewey licked his lips. 'The most interesting thing I've seen is that since you and Sheriff Morrison returned to town, you've been pacing around nervously as if you expect trouble.'

Gabriel rocked his head from side to side to give the impression that he was thinking about revealing something, and then shrugged and stood up straight.

'As you say, it sure is interesting, and the truth will come out before long.'

Gabriel tipped his hat to Dewey and turned to go.

'So there is a truth to come out?' Dewey called after him.

'More than one,' Gabriel said to himself and then turned and raised his voice. 'There is, so make sure you tell everyone about it, including Jim.'

'I sure will, but . . .' Dewey trailed off when he realized that he'd made a mistake by speaking without thinking. Then he made a second mistake by trying to cover up his blunder with a smile and a shrug. 'I'm sure my customers will be eager to hear about Nyle's death if that's what's happened.'

Gabriel considered Dewey as he took his time in replying to lengthen his discomfort.

'So you will tell Jim that it's over now?' he intoned.

Dewey shrugged. 'I just meant that I'll tell all my customers.'

'Your words sound plausible, but that look in your eye says otherwise.' Gabriel took a pace towards the bar. 'Where is he?'

Dewey opened and closed his mouth soundlessly, but a voice spoke up from the shadows beyond the stairs.

'You don't need to answer that,' the man said. 'He's figured it out.'

Gabriel turned to find a man was stepping into view. He had a gun drawn, but he held it low and he

148

had the same build as the man he'd seen on the night that Clyde and Warren had tried to kill Nyle.

'I assume you're Jim Albright,' he said.

'I am,' Jim said. 'And is Dewey's assumption that you've taken down Nyle King correct?'

Gabriel nodded. 'Nyle ambushed Sheriff Morrison and me in Jackson's Pass. We survived. He didn't.'

Jim looked aloft while taking deep breaths and then uttered a sigh of relief.

'Then you did well.'

'All we did was follow your leads while Nyle worried so much about what we'd find buried under the trading post that he showed his hand.'

Jim smiled. 'It's satisfying when a perfectly executed plan to take Nyle down one piece at a time works out.'

Jim tipped his hat and backed away towards the shadows, but Gabriel raised a hand.

'Your plan may have worked, but that doesn't mean that everything you did was justified. So you can't walk away from this without facing the consequences.'

Jim shrugged in an unconcerned manner, but then hardened his expression and aimed his gun at Gabriel's chest.

'I've done what I set out to do. Now I'll move on. If you try to stop me, I'll have to kill you.'

Dewey murmured in concern and edged towards Jim as if he was about to intervene, but when Jim shot him a warning glance he stopped moving.

'You've already killed enough,' Gabriel said. 'That stops here.'

'You shouldn't concern yourself with the men I've killed.' Jim gestured at Gabriel with his free hand. 'When you defeated Nyle, you probably had to kill more men than I did when I led him to you.'

'Maybe I did, but there's a difference. We defended ourselves while doing our duty as lawmen. You set out to kill purely for vengeance.'

Gabriel had spoken only to try to keep Jim talking, but to his surprise, his words felt more reasonable than he'd expected. For the first time, he entertained the thought of trying to arrest Jim rather than killing him, before dismissing the idea.

Jim sneered. 'If you've seen what's in the trading post, you know why I did it.'

'We found Bertha's body, so you had the right to seek vengeance, but the thing about vengeance is that it's not always effective. You can end up killing the wrong people.'

'I didn't,' Jim snapped.

'What about Deputy Edgar Newhall?'

'That was an accident.'

Gabriel shrugged. 'Maybe it was, but what

150

happened six months ago during Lorenzo Moretti's train raid?'

Jim opened his mouth to snap back another retort, but with a sigh he conceded Gabriel's point.

'That was a mistake. Marshal Caine appointed me as his deputy and told me to infiltrate Lorenzo's gang, but this low-life from Richland recognized me. I was forced to shoot him to maintain my cover. Then Lorenzo panicked and we left without stealing anything.'

Gabriel smiled as Jim's declaration connected the information that Nyle and Caine had given him. He spread his hands, using the motion to ensure that his right hand was close to his holster.

'Do you know the name of that low-life?'

'I was more concerned with making sure that Lorenzo didn't suspect my real identity. Then when Caine wasn't impressed with what I'd done, I had to keep out of his way while bringing down Nyle.' Jim considered Gabriel's firm-jawed expression. 'Who was he?'

'His name was Hugo Flynn. He was my brother and you gunned him down in cold blood, the same way you'll die.'

For long moments Jim looked Gabriel over and then appeared to dismiss the matter with a shrug.

'Telling me that was a mistake.' Jim pointed at

Gabriel's holster. 'Tip your gun on to the floor and kick it over here. Then I'm leaving. Don't come after me.'

CHAPTER 16

Gabriel settled his stance. Then he edged his hand towards his holster while shaking his head with a slow movement that showed he wouldn't comply with Jim's demand.

'You sure made a lot of mistakes during your quest for vengeance,' he said.

'I didn't!' Jim said.

His raised voice made Dewey twitch, suggesting he reckoned this confrontation would come to a head in the saloon. Jim glanced at him and smiled, showing that if Dewey was minded to reach for a gun beneath the bar, he was confident about whom he'd turn it on.

'You made the biggest mistake of all,' Gabriel said. 'You set out to destroy the wrong man.'

Jim shook his head. 'I didn't. Nyle killed Bertha.'

153

'He claimed he didn't. He accepted the other five bodies buried there were down to him, but not the woman's. I agree with him. He had no reason to kill her and I have every reason to think you connected the clues in the wrong way.'

Jim took a pace towards Gabriel, his eyes blazing and so Gabriel settled his stance and prepared to go for his gun.

'Linking them to Nyle was the only way they could connect,' Jim snapped. 'So amaze me. Who do you reckon did it?'

'You killed Orson Kemp and he sold goods of dubious quality.'

'He also had an unwelcome interest in Bertha and he told Harry Fink that she'd make a fine addition to the Red Night saloon. That means they were doing Nyle's bidding.'

'That doesn't have to point to Nyle. Clearly Orson often came in here to see her.' Gabriel shrugged as he struggled to think of any other valid explanations. 'And I guess Alvin Owens came in here to pick pockets before he was removed.'

Jim shook his head. 'Alvin didn't just steal valuables. He stole people, too. I reckon Harry hired him to kidnap her.'

'I didn't know that, but I still reckon you should have looked for other culprits, such as the people who came here.'

Dewey snarled with anger and ducked down before rising up with a six-shooter, which he aimed at Gabriel.

'Don't blame my saloon for being behind what happened to Bertha,' he said. 'Nyle killed her and that's the end of it.'

With two guns now aimed at him, Gabriel backed away for a pace, but he kept his hand beside his holster.

'I'm not blaming you, only someone who visited your saloon,' Gabriel said, but his comment didn't placate Dewey, who gestured at him with his gun.

'He won't let you leave, Jim,' he said. 'Kill him.'

'He has a good reason to want me dead,' Jim said. 'I won't shoot him unless he gives me no option.'

'He's already doing that!'

Jim glanced at Dewey. 'By insulting your customers?'

Dewey opened his mouth to reply, but then thought better of it and gave a shrug and a smile.

'Dewey knows,' Gabriel murmured as he recalled that Dewey had acted in the same sheepish manner when he'd caught him lying about the fact that he had helped Jim. He raised his voice. 'Dewey knows who Bertha's killer is!'

Jim glared at him, but then with a wince and a

155

quick turn of the head, he appeared to pick up on Gabriel's thoughts.

'Is that true?' Jim demanded.

'Ignore him,' Dewey said. 'He's just trying to distract you.'

'I know that, but answer my question. Did you know who did it all along? Did you only encourage me to think Nyle killed her so that I'd take on a man who owns the other saloons in town?'

'How could I know what happened to Bertha? She was one of my best saloon girls and what happened to her hurt me almost as much as it hurt you.'

'It couldn't have done, unless you knew her better than I thought.'

Jim narrowed his eyes as he appraised Dewey and in the silence Gabriel did the same. Dewey gulped and then with a roar of anger, he swung his free arm round to grip his wrist and steady his aim at Gabriel.

Before he could fire, Jim blasted a shot that caught Dewey in the side and made him stumble. His gun fell from his grasp and clattered on to the bar as he struggled to stay upright.

'I didn't mean to do it,' he said through gritted teeth.

'Are you talking about Bertha?' Jim demanded as he strode towards him. 'Did you kill her?'

Dewey murmured something, but the words were

unintelligible. Then his eyes glazed and he toppled over behind the bar.

Jim reached the bar and leaned over it, his scowl confirming that Dewey was dead. He slapped a fist against his thigh.

'His secrets probably died with him, but I reckon he did it,' Gabriel said. 'He must have worked out where Nyle hid bodies and buried her there to implicate him. Then he directed you to the post and let you reach your own conclusions.'

Jim straightened up, seemingly only then noticing that his attention had moved away from Gabriel. He swirled round, but it was to find that Gabriel had used the distraction to draw his gun and aim it at his chest.

'I got the revenge I wanted,' Jim said. 'It won't matter none to me if you take yours.'

Jim deposited his gun on the bar and raised his hands.

Gabriel firmed his gun arm, as he accepted that he'd also got everything he'd wanted to achieve. His finger tightened on the trigger, but only for a fraction before he stopped the movement.

'I'm a lawman now,' he said. 'I can't use that position for revenge.'

'Do it,' Jim said. 'Shoot.'

Jim rolled his shoulders, but when he looked at

him without fear in his eyes, Gabriel lowered the gun a mite.

'I won't end it this way.'

Jim frowned, seeming almost disappointed with his decision.

A steady handclap sounded in the doorway. Gabriel glanced over his shoulder and found that Morrison had arrived.

'That was the right decision,' he said.

Gabriel nodded and turned back to Jim. 'You knew he was there, didn't you?'

'Sure,' Jim said. 'I was interested to see what you did.'

'Then the fact that I didn't do what you wanted makes this all the better.' Gabriel gestured with his gun for Jim to head to the door. 'You are under arrest.'

'How long were you standing there?' Gabriel asked when Jim was locked up in a cell in a corner of the law office.

'I came when I heard the gunshot, so I only saw the ending to that confrontation,' Morrison said. 'I'm pleased you decided to let a court detail the full extent of Jim's activities.'

'Edgar's friends and family deserve to see justice done and my need for vengeance was no greater than theirs.' Gabriel sat down at his desk. 'But I won't deny that I was tempted to pull the trigger.'

'Of course you were, but you didn't and that's all that matters.' Morrison came over to Gabriel's desk and considered him. 'I know why you took this job, so I need to know what you want to do now.'

Gabriel stood up and headed to the window. It was early evening, but with the Silver Palace saloon and the Four Star saloon being closed tonight, the town was quiet.

'I never enjoyed being Marshal Caine's deputy because I only wanted to find my brother's killer, and I only became yours for the same reason.' Gabriel turned to Morrison. 'Now I'd like to find out what it's like being a deputy with no other motive in mind.'

'Then you'll get that chance and I reckon you're already finding out that delivering justice is more rewarding than delivering vengeance.'

'I know that now, although I've yet to find out if it's better than earning a bounty.'

Morrison narrowed his eyes, but Gabriel smiled and so he returned a smile. Then Morrison headed to the door and Gabriel joined him.

The two men stepped outside and looked up and down the darkening main drag.

'There's sure to be trouble before long,' Morrison said. 'So we need to be prepared to act, and this time we make sure that men like Nyle King don't get established.'

Gabriel nodded. Then they spent a few minutes enjoying the quiet until raised voices sounded in the distance, the voices becoming increasingly angry.

'And it sounds as if we're needed now,' Gabriel said.

'It sure does,' Morrison said. Then he set off towards the source of the noise. 'Come on. We have a job to do, Deputy.'